I0725602

This Book
Belongs To:

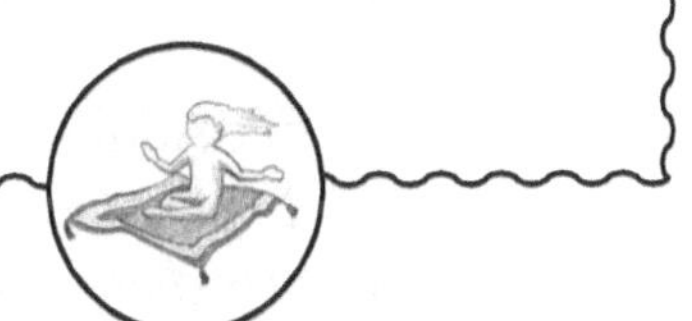

Book I
of the Agnes Kelly
Mystery Adventure Series

Book II
Narrow Escape in Norway

Book III
All is Revealed in Russia

Also by
Christine Keleny

For All Ages
The Red Velvet Box

Chakra wMagic

For Adults
Rosebloom
A Burnished Rose
Rose from the Ashes

Living in the House of Drugs

*Will the Real Carolyn Keene
Please Stand Up*

Intrigue in Istanbul

Book I

Christine Keleny

CKBooks

No parts of this book may be reproduced or used in any form without permission except for brief quotations used for articles or in reviews.

Contact Christine Keleny and see all of her books at: christinekelenybooks.com. ♦ Learn more about Agnes Kelly at: AgnesKellyMysteryAdventures.com

Publisher's Cataloging-In-Publication Data

Keleny, Christine.
  Intrigue in Istanbul / Christine Keleny.
    pages : illustrations ; cm. -- (An Agnes Kelly mystery adventure ; book 1)

    Summary: "A twelve year old girl (Agnes Kelly) goes to Istanbul with her grandmother after her father's funeral. There Agnes finds out that there is something suspicious about her father's death. The story takes place in 1961."--Provided by publisher.
  Interest age level: 007-012.
  Issued also as an ebook--ISBN: 978-0-9800529-6-1
  And a hardcover--ISBN: 978-0-9800529-5-4
  ISBN:978-1-949085-05-1

    1. Girls--Travel--Turkey--Istanbul--Juvenile fiction. 2. Fathers--Death--Juvenile fiction. 3. Intelligence officers--United States--Juvenile fiction. 4. Girls--Travel--Turkey--Istanbul--Fiction. 5. Fathers--Death--Fiction. 6. Spies--United States--Fiction. 7. Mystery fiction. 8. Adventure fiction. I. Title.
PZ7.1.K45 In 2016
[Fic]   2015920812

Published by CKBooks Publishing
P.O. Box 214
New Glarus, WI 53574
ckbookspublishing.com

Some fonts used courtesy of: "5th Grade Cursive" by Lee Batchelor, "Kingthings trypewriter" by Kevin King
The following images were used to create the drawings: taxi - 1974 Peter Loud, Bogart - 1941 AP photo, tour boat - akinci944, Hagia Sophia - Arild Vågen

Copyright 2016 Christine Keleny
All Rights Reserved

Dedicated to

Aaron
&
Rachel

with Love

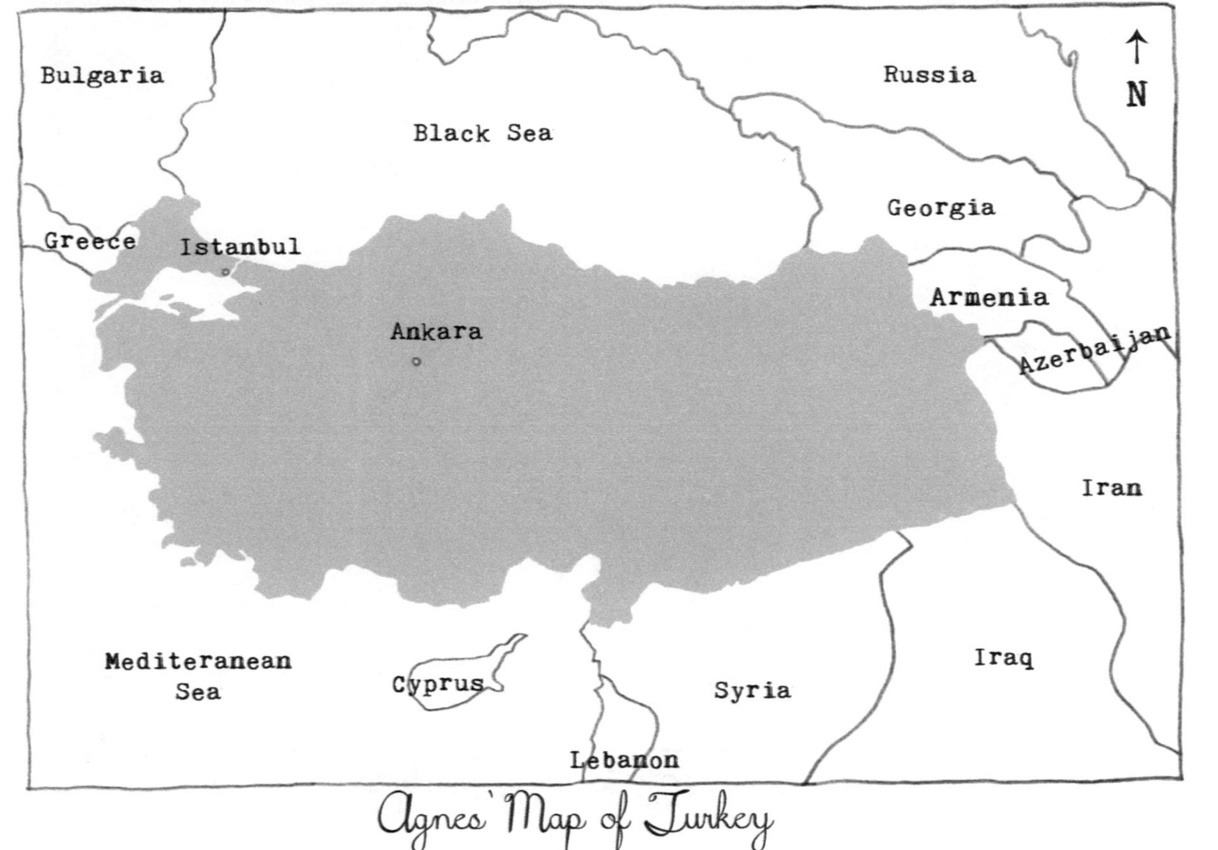

Agnes' Map of Turkey

Agnes' Map of Istanbul

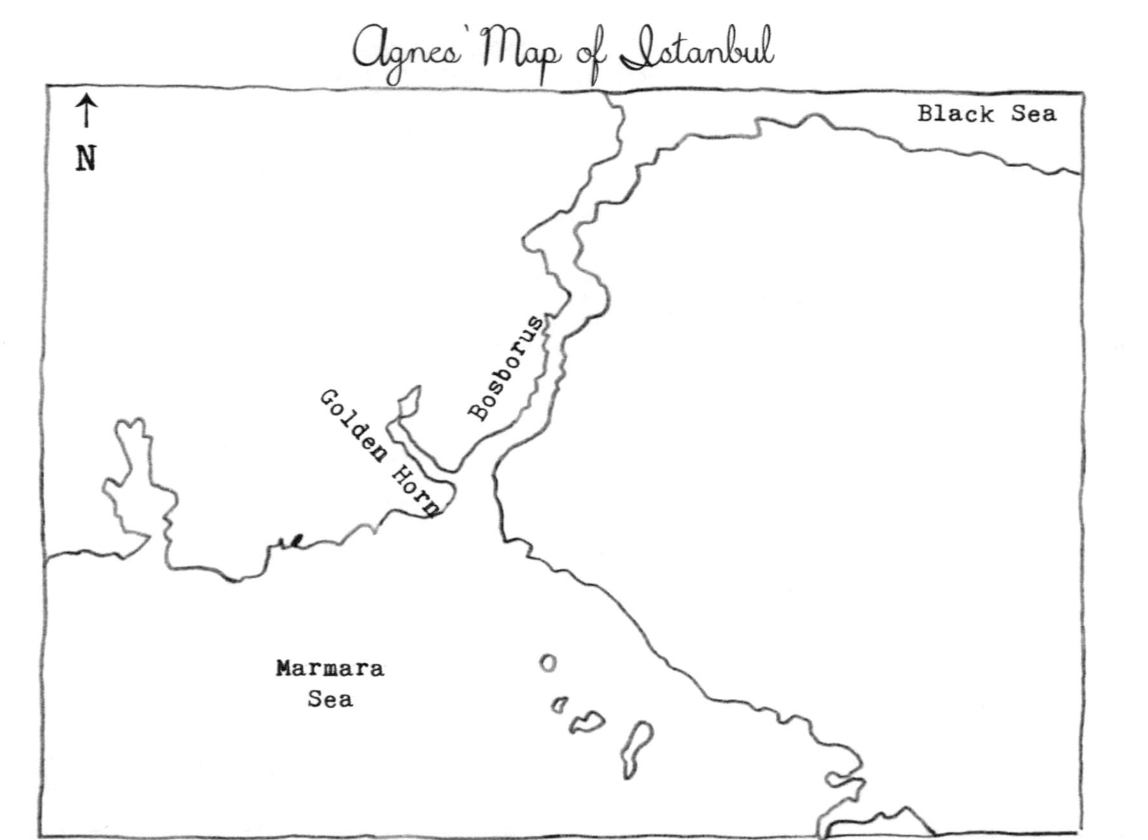

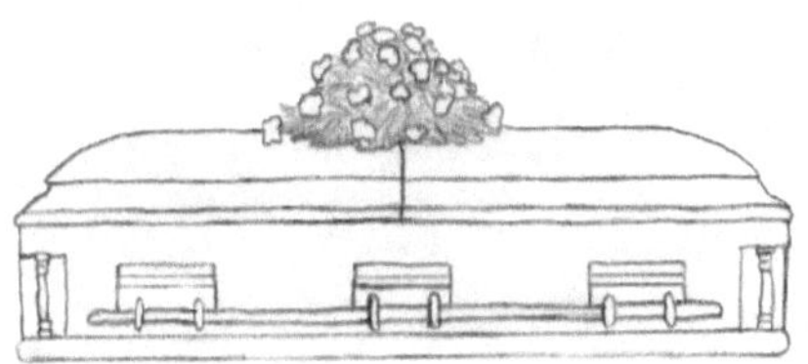

Chapter 1

It's really hot and tight in here; there's enough room to bring my hands up in front of my face, but that's about it. It doesn't matter though because I can't see them. I can't see anything. It's dark. I mean black. No, it's the definition of black. I've got this silky material all around me, and my head is even on a small silk pillow (or maybe fake silk. I wouldn't know the difference), but it's still hot in here, and I'm starting to get a little claustrophobic.

All this is mute. No, that's not it. What do adults say?...Moot! That's it! It's all a moot point because I'm dead.

Maybe I should start over and tell you what's going on here.

Okay, I'm not really dead, but I wish I were. I wish I were in that shiny, bronze-colored capsule I'm staring at and not my dad.

He died too young, or that's what I hear all the adults around me telling each other. Despite his prematurely gray hair, I'd have to agree with them on this point and I don't agree with adults on many things, believe me.

I didn't say that quite right. I should have said, 'Despite the fact that his hair WAS prematurely gray.' (I'm going to have trouble with the past tense thing for a while, I can tell.)

Considering the average life expectancy of an adult male in 1961 is 67.4, dying when you're forty-eight is early. I know this factoid, as my annoying oldest brother, Adam, would say, because I looked it up. Whatever I don't know, I look up. It's what I do. It drives my best friend, Margaret, wild. Whenever we're in the middle of the board game *Risk*, I'll run to our set of encyclopedias to check, say, Argentina, which claims to be where the tango was originated, but more importantly was the first country to use finger prints as a primary way to identify criminals. That was way, way, way back in 1892. In fact, it was first used this way after a really interesting case, a murder case to be exact, the murder of Francisca

Rojas's two children. I had to go to the library to find out this little interesting fact. (It's there. You can look it up yourself.) Who wouldn't want to run a country that was smart enough to use fingerprints to identify people? I always picked Argentina if Peg didn't get to it first.

But I digress [*v: to speak or write about something that is different from the main subject being discussed* – I looked it up in *Webster's*, of course], as our old, English (as in, he came right from England) neighbor Mr. Morrison always says. When you say "I digress," you have to hold out the "die" part of the word really long or it doesn't sound English enough. Peg and I are always trying to pretend we're sitting having tea with Mr. M. (We call Mr. Morrison, Mr. M. for short. It's just easier than Morrison), chatting about the Queen Mum or some such nonsense, using English accents and holding our little pinkies in the air ("chatting" is English, too, if you didn't know).

As I was saying, my father's death was too early. It was too early for me, too early for Danny, Peter, and Max (my three younger brothers), too early for Aaron (he's just two years older than me) and Adam and too early for Mom. (Yes, I am the only girl in my family, other than my mom.) For sure too early for her. Mom tries to be stoic [*adj: not affected by passion or feeling*] or tries to have a stiff upper lip, as Mr. M. would say. But I caught her crying one morning when I walked into the kitchen. I had gotten up unusually early during Easter break. I don't know about you, but when I don't have school, I stay in bed until at least nine just on principle. (I know, that's another adult word. But I like adult words. So sue me!) Even if I'm wide awake at eight or even, heaven forbid, seven. I'll just use the time constructively – as my mother would say – and get some good reading in. Mornings are a great time to read; the house is quiet and usually smells of coffee or, if I'm lucky, sausages.

Here I go digressing again. You'll see, I do that a lot. I'm supposed to be telling you about how I know my father's death is too early for my mom.

A

It was Easter break and I was walking into the kitchen way before I'm normally even awake. I was looking for a snack before breakfast. The room smelled great because Mom just made a pot of coffee. I don't like coffee, mind you; it tastes like burnt dirt. I just like the smell. She was standing in front of the coffee pot and it was percolating away just fine, but she was crying. She had one coffee cup on the counter in front of her, and her arm was outstretched and reaching into the cupboard, but she wasn't moving. It was like it was stuck there with Elmer's glue or something. She had her hand around another coffee cup and she was shaking so hard I thought she was going to drop it. I froze. I didn't know what to do. I had never seen my mother cry so hard in all my life. I mean she's a real sap when it comes to a sad story on one of those "made for TV" movies she likes to watch, and she even cried when we went to see the old film, Bambi, with my younger brothers when they were replaying it in the theater. I'd seen it before, of course, but I rarely turn down a chance to go to the movies, so I went along. Mom started blubbering partway through the movie. You know that part when the hunter kills Bambi's mother. It is kind of sad, even though they don't show the mom being killed. That would be too gross for kids to see. Not me, of course, but for little kids. You see, my dad hunts.

There I go again. My dad USED TO hunt. And when he'd bring home a dead deer and hang it up upside down in the garage, it wasn't a pretty sight, so I'm not squeamish. My mom would cry at stuff like that (not the dead deer in our garage, but the pretend dead deer that you didn't even see die!), but

I'd never seen her cry like that before. It was like something was breaking inside her that you couldn't see, and it really hurt as it was coming apart.

So I did what any self-respecting twelve-year-old would do. I backed out of the room as silently as I could.

A

I take in a deep breath and look over at my mother in our pew. Father Michael is waving an incense burner over Dad's coffin as he moves silently around it saying something in Latin that I can't quite catch. I make a mental note to look up the Catholic rights of the dead when I make my next trip to the library. I wonder if they'll have that sort of thing at the De Soto Public Library. (De Soto, Wisconsin is where I live. You know, the "Dairy State.") I may have to ask Father Michael if I can't find it at the library. I'll have to bring along my book of Latin so I can translate it if it's not written in English.

I know what you're thinking: Latin?!

Yes, I have a book of Latin proverbs. I asked for it for Christmas last year. Mr. M. is always spouting off Latin phrases when he's trying to confuse us kids (and my parents, too, by the look on their faces), so

I decided I'd show him that all kids in the good old U S of A aren't idiots, by learning a few Latin phrases myself. Mr. M's favorite is *Carpe diem* (pronounced car-pay dee-um). I could have almost figured out the *diem* part (meaning *day*) but I had to look up *carpe*. The whole thing means "Seize the day!" That's a pretty good one, I have to admit. My latest favorite is *Cum grano salis* (kum gra-no saa-lis). I like it because it's easy to remember and, like anything Latin, it makes you sound smarter than you really are. I'll use it in a sentence and then you'll figure it out right away: "You have to take what my older brother says cum grano salis."

Did you get it? "With a grain of salt."

I'm not exactly sure what it means other than my dad used to say it about our Uncle Bob (one of his younger brothers) when he talked about all the things he did in the big war or, come to think of it, he said that about most anything Uncle Bob said. I think it means he's full of beans or something like that. Uncle Bob tells some pretty big tales.

You might think I sound kind of cold hearted with all this talk about board games and Latin words, but I'm not. I brought Kleenex in my purse (my only purse, mind you) because I never know when the tears will come out of nowhere. I mean almost nowhere. (Though I looked that up too. The human body produces tears by stimulating two glands called lacrimal glands, which are behind the upper eyelids. These glands excrete – isn't that a deliciously disgusting word – lacrimal fluid, the medical term for tears. Lacrimal fluid is very salty, although there is some evidence that the level of salt changes depending on the cause of the tears. Isn't that fascinating?!) [Note to self: check salt level in tears created for various reasons.]

I cried, of course, when Mom first told us kids the news. It has seemed too weird most of the rest of the time, though, like Dad has gone on one of his work trips to some place like Britain or Russia, and he'll be home in a week or so with a set of Russian nesting dolls or some English chocolate, with a great story about it. But this last work trip has been really long, and I'm starting to understand that he's really not coming home this time. My brain knows the facts but somehow it still doesn't seem real. His last trip was to England, then Turkey and Mom said someone hit the car he was driving. She said it wasn't his fault, but you know how they drive on the other side of the road over there, he could have easily made a mistake. I know I would for sure, that is, if I could drive.

Maybe if it was an open casket, like at Grandma Barb's funeral, we'd see him super still and cold like Grandma was (I touched her hand when my parents weren't watching. I had to do it just to see. You understand, right?!) But Mom wouldn't let us see Dad's body. She said they embalmed him and everything, but still, she wanted us to "remember him like he was when he was with us."

As interesting as the whole embalming thing is (I looked that up, too. It takes two gallons of formaldehyde to embalm an adult. Check the facts for yourself.), I didn't argue the point as I normally might have done. Seeing a frog in Mr. Pearson's science room in a bottle of fluid is one thing. Seeing your own father in a similar state, is quite another.

A

We all stand for one more hymn, "Abide With Me." My mother wordlessly shoves a songbook into my hands. My brothers she ignores, but me, she expects to sing. I like singing generally (Elvis the pelvis, as Aaron likes to call him, Patsy Cline, or Chubby Checker) but solemn church songs – not so much.

I have a hard time finding the pages of the

hymn with my white gloves on. *Yes*, I am wearing white gloves, because "that is what young ladies do," according to my mother. I suppose I should try and be more lady-like, but it just doesn't come naturally for me. Peggy, she was born a girl. Me...I suspect I am just a boy in a girl's skin. It's not that I want to be a boy. Boys...well, explaining how boys are and how I wouldn't be caught dead being one would be a whole lot of pages in and of itself. Let's just say, I think I was born to improve the work we women get delegated [v: *to choose someone to do something*] to do, and I've got some big plans for us, ladies, so hold on to your hats!

Halfway into the song my eyes start to fill with tears, so I blink as fast as I can and touch my hand to my heart to feel the small, oval piece of metal next to my skin. It's an honest to goodness Saint Christopher medal. My dad used to wear it in the big war – WWII, of course. Mom thought I might like to have it, and she was right. She's pretty smart sometimes, for a mother, anyway. Grandma Agnes Kelly, my dad's mom and my namesake, told us my dad signed up to go fight in the war, he didn't wait to be drafted like some of them. He was an airplane pilot. She was pretty proud of him, but mostly I think she was glad that he made it back home. Me too! He's...he WAS a pretty swell dad.

When the song is finally over, we're supposed to file out. Adam, being sixteen, gets to be one of the pallbearers. Aaron wanted to be a pallbearer too, but Mom said he wasn't old enough since he's only fourteen. As it is, I can see Adam, in his oversized suit coat, straining under the weight. There are five other men helping lift the casket off its perch, but still, that copper colored thing looks like it weighs a ton. [Note to self: find out the weight of an average casket.]

Grandma Agnes and some of her grown kids (my aunts and uncles) are sitting in the pew just opposite ours. Now Grandma is standing, staring at me as I stand staring at her, not sure what to do. Mom's already stepped out into the aisle, behind the casket. Grandma Agee, as we call her, has the oddest expression on her face before she finally steps out of the pew after Mom. She isn't perturbed [*v: to cause to be worried or upset*] by my indecision; it is more like something has just dawned on her.

It is a dreary and blustery May day outside, so I have to hold down my Easter hat – last year's model, a white, fake straw number with pink and blue ribbons around the band that trail down the back of my head – to keep it from blowing off as we stand in our good shoes in the trampled grass at the gravesite. I don't wobble on spikey heels like most of the ladies in the crowd, but I have on my white satin Easter shoes, and I'm not sure I'm going to be able to get the stains out. My first communion shoes were white patent leather, which would have worked much better under the current circumstances, but Peggy told me only little girls wore patent leather anymore and I'm practically a woman, so that was out.

Grandma Agee is next to Mom because it's her son that's in the casket, so she gets front row privileges like all us kids and Mom. The aunts and uncles from both sides of the family are behind us. Dad's got only one older sibling [*n: one of two or more individuals having one common parent*], Aunt Mary, then he's got scads of younger ones, including a few who still live in Ireland, where most of them were born. Mom's older sister Millie is here too and her two brothers. Funerals are like live genealogy lessons; you get to learn who you're related to and, if you listen closely, you get to find out a few interesting family facts at the same time. I learned the first juicy tidbit just a few minutes ago.

⅄

"Uncle Bob sure gets cold easy," Aaron said as we were walking up the hill to the gravesite. "His nose is always red."

"He's not cold, you idiot, he's a drunk," Adam informed us. "That's what happens when people drink too much."

I turned around and looked at Uncle Bob. He saw me looking at his Rudolph nose and gave me a wink. If he was drunk, he is a pretty friendly drunk.

⚘

"Now, if you would like, you can take a flower as a memorial to our beloved Patrick," Father Michael says to the crowd.

I feel a hand on my back as my mom pushes me forward. She steps closer and pulls a rose out of the carpet of red and green that covers Dad's coffin.

"Go ahead, Agnes," she says, so I pick a rose too. It's the deepest red I've ever seen and velvety as a ripe peach. I put it up to my nose so I can feel the petals against my skin and I pick up just a hint of a scent, like laundry fresh off the line but a touch sweeter. Danny and Peter take one too, but the other boys notice it's mostly the ladies that have flowers, so they just walk away with their hands in their coat pockets. Everyone is standing around like they're lost, but Peggy spies me and runs over. She stops right in front of me and without warning, wraps her arms around me.

"I thought you might like a hug."

"Yeah, I guess. Thanks."

I'm not a big hugger and Peggy knows this, but it's been a weird day all around, so I just take it in stride.

We turn to stroll down the hill toward the waiting cars. There is an awkward silence between us that neither of us seems to know how to break.

"You coming to the luncheon?" I finally ask.

"You mean people eat after funerals? I thought they just went home and sat around talking in whispers the rest of the day."

"Yeah, of course they do. Aaron says it's an old sin-eater thing, but I think he's just read one too many comic books. *I* think it's a church lady thing. It's the only way they know how to make someone feel better," I say as if I'm the expert, an expert of one – my grandma Barb's funeral – but that's one more than Peggy, so in this case, I am. "There's all kinds of stuff to choose from, so usually you can find a couple things that are edible." I start to pick up my pace just thinking of the platters of ham sandwiches made on small square buns, crusty casseroles of hot creamy potatoes, and pan after pan of desserts all waiting on tables back in St. James' basement. Peggy quickens her steps to keep up.

A

I put my plate down in front of me at an empty table. Peggy and I were third and fourth in line behind Max and Aaron. I had to help Danny, since he's only four, so Peter had to wait behind us. Adam is too cool to rush for the food, even though he can pack it away with the best of them. Besides a couple little ham sandwiches (just as I predicted), I nabbed some cherry Jell-O with whipped cream on top, a rice crispy bar and something that looks like a chocolate chip cookie but was baked in a square pan. I by-passed the green bean casserole and the creamed peas since Mom is too busy talking with friends and relatives to make sure I have a balanced meal.

Peggy and I dig right in with ne'er a word between us (Ne'er is short for never. I heard Mr. M. say that once and I think it's kinda cool, so I use it when I can). The quiet doesn't last long, however.

"You must be Agnes," a big lady in a dark purple dress says as she touches me on the shoulder.

"Huh?" I mumble, my mouth full of ham and bun.

"You probably don't remember me, but I'm your mother's best friend, Jane Parker. Well, I was Jane Marshall when your mother and I played together." She picks up my hair and bounces it in her hands as if she wants to take a hunk home for herself. I notice her hair is looking a little thin, so I turn around in an exaggerated way so I can pull it out of her sweaty hands without being rude. "You look just like your mom when she was your age, the curly brown hair and all."

I try and envision this lady when she was twelve and I just can't do it. She's three feet wide, okay, maybe just two, but in my mind her girth and the purple dress are too imposing [*adj: very large or impressive*] to be able to shrink to a size eight-miss.

"You made it, Jane," my mother says, coming up behind her and giving her a polite hug.

"Of course, Bubbles. Nothing could have stopped me," she says, still holding onto my mother. "I'm so sorry."

Bubbles? Did she just call my mother Bubbles? My mouth is hanging open, and I try to shut it before the Jell-O I just took a bite of comes jiggling out.

My mother sees me gaping, but she diverts her

attention to my plate of food as if her friend hadn't said anything strange. She furrows her brow at the assortment, gives me a disapproving look, but doesn't say a thing. Ah, the benefits of a crowd full of relatives and friends!

She turns back to her friend. "We'll have to talk later," she says, in almost a conspiratorial tone [*conspiratorial, adj: involving a secret plan by two or more people to do something that is harmful or illegal: of or relating to a conspiracy*]. I can almost see my mom and Jane huddled together on the church playground, heads bent close, whispering secrets to each other like Peggy and I do. Then Mom gets pulled away by someone else, and we're left in peace again.

"Did she call your mother *Bubbles*?" Peggy asks.

"That's what I heard," I say, shrugging my shoulders. Then I turn my attention back to more important matters, my food. That is until I feel another poke. I turn to look but the person has already walked around me. I swing back around and Grandma Agee is setting her plate down next to Danny.

"Mind if I join ya?" she says, sitting down.

I guess it doesn't matter what I think because she's joining us anyway. Actually, I don't mind

Grandma Agee. She's got a cool accent, like Mr. M. but hers is from Ireland, where she lived most of her life.

I know, I say "cool" a lot. I guess I picked that up from Adam. He says it a lot too, but mostly when he's talking about music – his most favorite thing – or girls – his second most favorite thing.

I expect her to start talking, asking me how school is going, what I like to do for fun, what I'm going to do this summer...stuff adults always ask kids, but she doesn't say a thing. She just eats her food in peace and quiet like the rest of us at the table.

Peggy pokes me under the table and tips her head ever so slightly in Grandma Agee's direction. She thinks it's weird too. My eyes go wide in an "I don't know" expression and we set back to eating and watching the crowd, saving up our observations and things we've overheard to share when we're alone.

The tranquil [*adj: quiet and peaceful*] scene is disturbed once again when a bunch of my dad's brothers and sisters sit down too. With Grandma Agee's kids all sitting down next to each other, I can see the family resemblance. They all have the same light skin and freckles that dad had, though I think Aunt Sharon has covered hers up with a ton of makeup. Most of them have the same light or red-tinted hair, except Aunt Mary; she looks like she got drenched in water from a very rusty downspout. Peggy would say that it came from a bottle.

Grandma Agee looks up when her kids sit down, but doesn't say anything until she notices someone is missing. "Sean, go get your brother, Bobby."

"Hello, Agnes," Mary says as she puts her napkin in her lap. "And how is Danny doing?"

Danny looks at Aunt Mary as if she just spoke Martian or something then looks at me for interpretation.

"He doesn't talk much," I tell her. "He's only four."

"Ah, yes, four," she says, as if that explains it all, then she turns her attention to Peggy. "And are you a friend of Agnes'?"

Peggy gives me the same expression as Danny, but I kick her under the table, letting her know that I only interpret Martian for little kids; she's old enough to answer for herself.

"Yes," Peggy finally gets out. But that is the extent of it.

"Well, pleased to meet you. It's nice of you to be here for Agnes."

Peggy nods her head and drops it back down to stare at her food. My friend, who normally hardly shuts up, is suddenly speechless. I have to grin at her red cheeks.

"Do both of you girls go to St. James?" Mary asks.

But before either of us can answer, Grandma Agee speaks for us. "For God's sake, Mary, leave the girls be, can't ya see they just want ta eat."

My mouth is hanging open again and I have to make an effort to shut it. I didn't know grown kids got in trouble with their mothers too.

Not a word more is spoken at the table until Uncle Sean sits down, then Uncle Bob, who sits right next to his mother.

"A meal fit for a king!" Uncle Bob says, and he says it so loud I think the whole dining hall can hear him. He almost tips his very full plate over as he tries to set it down. "Whoops-a-daisy!" he says with a laugh.

Grandma Agee is boring two holes through his head with her eyes, but he doesn't seem to notice. Everyone else at the table looks politely away or just ignores him. Danny, Peggy, and I are mesmerized [*v: to hold someone's entire attention*].

A church lady arrives in a crisp, frilly pink

apron with a coffee pot in hand. "Would anyone like some coffee?"

Most of the adults turn over their cups and get filled up. "Just half a cup for me, if ya don't mind," Uncle Bob says. Then once the lady has stepped away, he pulls a thin, metal container from his breast pocket and pours some clear liquid into the cup until it's full.

"Do you have to, Bobby?" Grandma Agee says.

"I'm still jet-lagged, Mother. If I'm gonna sit through all this chit-chattin' and hand-shakin', I need somethin' ta lift me spirits," he says and takes a big sip. Uncle Bob has the same accent as his mother.

He seems to spy me over the rim of his cup. "Well, you must be Patrick's Agnes," he says with a warm smile. "I'd know you a mile away."

I can't help myself, but I smile back and nod. Of course, he really wouldn't be able to make me out if we were standing a mile apart. Probably the only thing he could tell is that I was wearing a dress, but it's one of those many "figures of speech" that adults like to use. I'm sure you've heard your share too: six of one, half dozen of another; that's the pot calling the kettle black; and the always confusing, that's neither here nor there. What the heck is that supposed to mean? Anyway, I'm digressing again.

What happens next is amazing and funny at the same time. Uncle Bob stands up and reaches over the table to give me a hardy handshake, letting his tie fall in his food in the process. Danny giggles.

Uncle Bob looks down and laughs along with him. "Just testin' the food," he says, wiping it off with his napkin. "If it goes up in flames, then I know it's too hot ta eat."

He winks at Danny, which makes him giggle even more.

Uncle Bob starts in on his food, shoveling it in like there's no tomorrow. But he still manages to talk between mouthfuls. "You know your daddy was quite the bookworm when he was a kid," he says, pointing to the book I have next to me on the table. I always carry a book with me to social functions, in case I get bored and I want something to do.

I look up from my rice crispy bar. I haven't seen much of my dad's family because they all live on the east or west coast or over in Ireland, so I know very little about them or about my dad when he was young. "What did he like to read?" I ask, interested in any shred of information about my father's past.

"Spy and detective stories mostly. I think his favorites were the Jonathan Latimer stories, but he liked Dashiell Hammett, too and good old Sherlock Holmes, a course."

"I've never heard of Jonathan Latimer or Dashiell Hammett," I say.

"Probably before your time," Bob says and downs a big gulp of his special coffee. "Not too surprising then that he got into..."

And without warning Grandma Agee stands up, hitting Uncle Bob's arm and cutting him off in mid-sentence. "Robert," she says through tight lips, as if she's afraid her false teeth are going to fall out, "have ya seen what the lovely ladies have made for pie?"

Uncle Bob looks at her strangely. "I've got half a plate a food yet...."

But Grandma Agee interrupts him again, this time picking him up by the lapel of his suit jacket and pulling him to standing. "But you wouldn't want to be waitin' 'til it's all gone, now would ya?" she says and pushes him in the direction of the dessert table.

Everyone at the table is as surprised by Grandma's little maneuver as I am, but I'm not looking at my relatives or even at Peggy, I've got my eyes glued on Grandma Agee. She's reading Uncle Bob the riot act over at the dessert table – that's another one of those sayings I'm not quite sure where it came from, but basically, it means he's getting an ear full, and you don't have to be a genius to understand what that means. I'm concentrating hard on Grandma's face, specifically her lips. But she's turned ever so slightly away from me so I can only make out a bit of what she's saying: "I told ya..." and "...button your lip" among the finger wagging and eye scowling she's giving poor Uncle Bob.

With Grandma's odd reaction and my dad being gone, unable to explain himself to me ever again, I feel an urgent need to find out what in the world he "got into" that Grandma Agee doesn't want me to know about.

Chapter 2

Most everyone has left now. Mom's in the kitch-
en thanking the church ladies and Grandma Agee is
sitting on one of the extra church pews that rests
along the entrance wall to the church basement, or
what I know as our lunch room. She's going home
with us tonight, mother insisted. We don't really
have room for any of Dad's family to stay at the
house, but we're making room for Grandma Agee
and I suspect I know just where.

I'm watching Peter antagonizing [*v: to irritate or
upset someone*] Danny, making sure he doesn't take
it too far and get Mom upset. She doesn't need to
deal with Danny crying on a day like today. I can
tell she's tired because she's leaning on the door jam,

shifting her weight from one foot to the other. My mom wears heels when she goes out of the house, like most ladies do, but it's four o'clock and she's been in them all day. I took mine off an hour ago and my heels are only a half an inch high. Grandma Agee catches my eye and waves me over. Of course, she doesn't actually "catch my eye." Both of my eyes are still in my head. It's just another one of those sayings. [Note to self: Find out where "catch my eye" and "read the riot act" came from.]

I make my way over toward my Granny. Maybe I can think of a way to ask her about what Uncle Bob said.

"Agnes, I wanted to ask ya somethin' before your mother comes over," she says in a rather serious tone. Grandma Agee is sixty-seven, which is kind of old, but you wouldn't know it by looking at her. First off, she is a lot thinner than most of the ladies her age in our church, which are really the only old people I know. Way, way, way back, De Soto used to be a really busy place. De Soto is on the Mississippi River and it used to get a lot of traffic from the river and the railroad that still runs right alongside it. There were a lot of Germans and Norwegians in town and those folks like to cook. That's why I can hardly move, my dress is so tight. Secondly, Grandma Agee dresses more like my mom than my grandma Barb did when she was alive. Like today, she's got on a gray dress, but a nice tube shaped number with a small collar accented in black with matching pockets and five sets of black buttons down the front for decoration. Not that I pay attention to such things, but Peggy made a special point to compliment me on how nice my Granny looked. Grandma Agee has gray hair, but she keeps it in a loose bun at the back of her head, not in the typical tight-curled helmet that looks like washed-out cotton candy that most older ladies wear.

"When are ya done with school?" she asks.

"You mean for the summer?"

"Yes."

"Three weeks and two days," I say with certainty. When Easter break rolled around, I started counting the days. It's not that I don't like school. I like it a lot; it's just that I like summer break more. I can learn about the stuff I want to learn about in the summer, not just the stuff I *have* to learn about when I'm in school.

"How would you like to leave school a little early this year?"

I straighten up and my eyes are now glued to her face (Of course, my eyes aren't stuck on my grand-mother's face. It's another one of those sayings, and it means I'm staring hard at her). "Sure! Why?" I say.

"I'm takin' a little trip and I need some company. Plus, I thought you'd like a little time away from all your brothers," she says as a paper airplane made out of a pink placemat goes flying by, immediately followed by Max and Peter with Danny bringing up the rear shouting, "Make me one! Make me one!"

"That'd be swell, but I'm not sure Mom will go for it."

"Leave your mother ta me," Grandma says with certainty, and from her determined expression, I have little doubt she is going to get her way.

With the news that I might be going on a trip with Grandma, I completely forget about asking her about what Uncle Bob was going to say about my dad.

A

It takes Grandma a whole week to bring up the trip idea with my mother. I think she wanted to give Mom some time to get her head on straight, since she's been kind of all over the place since dad died.

And with Grandma staying with us a few days, I figured I'd get to ask her what Uncle Bob was going to say about my dad. I try talking to her a couple times, but the minute I say anything about him, she immediately changes the subject, like it hurts her too much to talk about him or something. I can understand. I figure I'll have some time on our trip to try asking her again, so I decide to just wait. Mom says as time passes, it will hurt less to have dad gone, but I'm not so sure. After a week, it still feels the same for me.

Oh, by the way, I went to the library and Mrs. Prichard, one of the librarians, told me that "catch my eye" – *to get someone's attention* – and "reading someone the riot act" – which means *to warn or scold someone severely* – are called idioms, and there is a whole book of them. She showed it to me! To read someone the riot act was taken from a 1715 law in England that said that *people committing a riot had to stop within an hour of the magistrate reading the act (or law) that said you can't riot.* I spent a whole hour reading the idioms and writing down the more useful ones in my composition notebook. Getting your head on straight wasn't in the book, but I would guess it was taken from "getting your head together," which *was* in the book.

The Sunday before Grandma is going to leave, Mom tells everyone there is going to be a family meeting. This makes us all a little nervous since during the last family meeting, Mom told us that Dad had died. When I tell Grandma Agee about Mom's little pow-wow, she decides that will be a good time to tell the family about our trip. But before Grandma can say anything, Mom has a bombshell of her own to drop – dropping a bombshell is another idiom and dates back to WWI. It means *to make an unexpected or shattering announcement.*

"I've gathered all you children together because I have something important to tell you."

Mom hesitates, and we all look at each other, trying to figure out who else could have died.

"I've decided to go back to work," she says and gives us a weak smile.

I look around at the blank looks on my brothers' faces and realize nobody is going to say anything, so I decide to speak up. I say what I know everyone is thinking. "You used to work?"

Mom crosses her ankles and takes a deep breath, but it is my grandma who answers my question.

"Believe it or not, children, your mother had a life before ya came along."

My mother gives Grandma Agee another weak smile. "I was a high school English teacher," she says.

We're all still dumbfounded [*adj: very shocked or surprised*], but I can't help but be proud of my mom. Though I'm still not sure she's right in the head. Who's going to help my idiot brothers with their homework? Who's going to cook meals and clean the house? Who's going to make our lunches each morning? The minute the questions run through my head, I am sure I know the answer. I swallow hard, kissing my trip with my grandmother goodbye. But then Mom says something else I didn't expect.

"I won't start working until this fall; I have to take a few classes this summer to get caught back up," she says. "And in order for me to be able to go to class and have time to study, your Aunt Millie has agreed to come and live with us for a while. Well, Aunt Millie and her maid."

Everyone looks at each other with the same vacant look on their faces. Our Aunt Millie lives in Washington D.C. She was married to an older looking guy named Donald, who died just a couple years ago. They never had kids, but they must have been rich because she lives in a really big house on the edge of the city, and she has her own maid and grounds keeper. I've never been there myself, I've just seen a picture of her and her husband standing in front of a boxy-looking house Mom said was built in the colonial times.

"We're gonna get a maid?" Peter says.

Mom squirms in her chair. "She's not our maid, Peter. She works for your aunt and Aunt Millie doesn't seem to be able to let her go, so she's coming to stay with us."

"She told me at the funeral she has someone who mows her lawn for her. Is she gonna bring him too?" Max says with hope in his voice. Anything to get out of mowing the lawn or really, get out of doing anything that even looks like work is right up Max's alley.

"No, it's just the maid," Mom says with finality. "The grounds keeper has to stay and watch over her house."

"Well, that's good," Grandma Agee says quite loudly, "because I would like ta take Agnes with me ta Istanbul."

Boom! There goes another bomb in the room. Everyone turns to face Grandma.

"I meant ta say somethin' to you earlier, Mary, but now is as good a time as any," she says, then stands and walks over by me as if we both had this planned a long time ago.

I'm actually in shock. I can feel the color drain from my face, and I can hardly catch my breath. *Istanbul! I didn't know she was planning on going to Istanbul!* I'm not even sure I know where Istanbul is!

"Why are you taking Agnes to Turkey?" my mother asks, answering at least part of my question.

I snap my head in Grandma's direction since I'm just as interested in her answer as my mother is.

"I have...I need..." Grandma Agee seems stumped by the question. Her brow furrow gets deeper the more she thinks about it. "I want some company," is what she finally gets out. Now Grandma almost looks like she's mad with my mother for asking why she wants to take her only daughter to some foreign country. "The girl has fended for herself with all these boys for twelve years, Mary; I think she deserves some time away."

I snap my head back to face my mother. She's looking at Grandma Agee and me as if she is going to say something but she doesn't quite know how to say it. She shuts her mouth and looks at my brothers, then finally back to Grandma and me. "How long are you planning on being gone?"

I jump up and run over to my mother, wrapping my arms around her neck. I hold on tight until she eventually wraps her arms around me too. I hear my brothers grumbling in the background, but I easily ignore them.

I'm going to Istanbul, Turkey!

I just have to find out where Turkey is!

Λ

Peggy's on her stomach on my pink chenille bedspread with *Modern Travel in the Twentieth Century*, *Travelers Guide to Turkey*, and *Istanbul: A Cultural History* – books I recently got out of the library – all around her. I have to take a moment to explain the pink bedspread. I asked for a chenille one for my birthday because Peggy has one and they are really soft to lie on. The fact that it's pink is my mother's idea. I think it's her hope that if she gives me enough girlie things, I'll start acting more like a girl. It hasn't worked so far, but she keeps trying.

Peggy has our encyclopedia of the letter T open in front of her. She's reading it out loud while I pack. I've already read it, twice.

"It says here that Turkey is considered the

meeting point of two continents. What continents are those?"

"Europe and Asia," I say.

Peggy goes back to reading. "The current population is 1.3 million and has a land mass of 297,591 square miles."

"That's bigger than Texas," I add for clarification.

Peggy continues. "The capital is Ankara..."

"That's kind of in the center of the country, but Istanbul is actually bigger," I inform her. "I don't know why Istanbul isn't the capital anymore, in fact it used to be the capital of the whole Roman Empire when they called it Constantinople, but Ankara was probably where some sultan was born or something, so he picked that as the new capital."

Peggy's eyes shoot above the top of the encyclopedia. "They have sultans?! Like in the Arabian Nights?! Neat!" (Peggy uses "neat" a lot.)

I have no idea if any of the Turkish sultans had anything to do with picking the capital, of course, but since the country I'm going to travel to used to be run by a sultan, I thought I'd throw that little tidbit into the conversation. "They used to. They don't anymore."

"That's too bad," Peggy says, then drops her head back into the book. "Its main language is

Turkish and the main religion is Islam." Peggy looks back up at me as I rummage through my sock drawer trying to find matching pairs of knee socks that don't have any holes in them. I found only three pair so far, and past that, I'm not having much luck. "Islam, what's Islam?"

"I really don't know much about that religion. It's on my new list of books to check out. The only thing I know is that they worship in mosques."

Ready to give up on the sock mystery, I turn and pick up the book on Istanbul. I go to the first page I marked with a little scrap of paper – having been cured of the habit of dog-earing book pages back when I was, like, five – and I lie down on my stomach next to Peggy.

"Look at this!" I say with excitement. I open to the chapter titled *Must See Sights* and turn to the second page: *Museums*. Above the text is a picture of a large, brick, tan-colored structure with four sides of equal length. There are tall, thin towers at each corner called minarets, which make it look like something out an Arabian tale. The center of the building is dominated by a massive dome that is perched above the rest of the structure. "This is called the Hagia Sophia, which means Holy Wisdom. It was first built in *anno domini* 537 as a Greek Christian church."

Peggy rolls her eyes. "Okay, miss Latin, what's *anno domini*?"

"In the year of our Lord."

"Holy mackerel! Five-thirty-seven was a long time ago! How'd they manage to build that?"

"Probably poor laborers, like they used in Egypt to build the pyramids."

Peggy and I know a bit about the Egyptians because we learned about them in Bible study at school – a daily requirement at St. James.

"I don't know Greek churches or anything but that doesn't look like any church I've seen," Peggy says.

"That's because of those four pointy towers. They're called minarets. They were added in 1453 by Sultan Mehmed II when he took over the city and turned it from a Christian church into an Islamic mosque."

I flip to my next scrap-paper bookmark. "Look at this!" I turn the book so Peggy can see the men all dressed in white: white shirts, white pants, white long-sleeved jackets, and floor-length white skirts. The only thing that isn't white is a wide, black cloth waistband and a tall, brown tubular hat on their heads.

"Who are those guys and why are they wearing skirts!?" Peggy said with a touch of shock in her voice.

"They are called Whirling Dervishes, and I'm not sure why they're wearing skirts." I look at the picture myself and contemplate [*v: to think deeply or carefully about something*] her question. The picture has the men all turning in place, which causes their skirts to spread out in a wide circle from their waists.

"I suppose it's the same reason we like to twirl in our poodle skirts; because it looks cool."

Peggy nods, understanding my logic. "Now I know why my mother calls me a whirling dervish when I do that. I thought she was just making that up."

Peggy picks up the book on airplanes. "I can't believe you're going to fly there," she says, leafing through the book of sleek, silver prop planes and larger white jetliners with colored logos of Pan Am, Northwest or TWA plastered on their sides and tails. "You gonna take one of these prop jobs, like in that Bogart movie we saw last week? What was the name of that film?"

"Casablanca," I say, taking the book from her. "And that was set in WWII. Remember the Nazi guy?"

"Oh yeah."

I find a picture of a long jet plane and give the book back to Peggy. "We're gonna take one like this, though I don't know what exact plane." I go back to looking through my book on Istanbul. "Grandma Agee says we're flying with Pan Am."

"Neat," Peggy says, giving a onceover to the lovely flight attendant, who is wearing a Jackie O pill hat (Jacqueline Kennedy Onassis for the boys out there – hint: the president's wife). The flight attendant is also wearing a perpetual smile [*perpetual, adj: continuing forever or for a very long time*], which I find out later is really how it is! Peggy tips her head slightly and tries to imitate her. "Maybe that's what I could be when I grow up, a flight attendant. Then I could fly to really neat places for free!"

I nod my head. That sounds like a perfect job for Peggy. "I'll check 'em out for you on my trip."

⋀

It took us forever to get to O'Hare airport in Chicago. Everyone came along, of course, since I am the first one in our family, other than my mother, who has ever flown before, so they all wanted to see what it was all about. Even Adam wanted to come once he saw the Pan Am brochure Grandma had given me with the cute flight attendant on the front. My guess is he wanted to see one up close.

The nice lady at the Pan Am desk makes small talk with me and Grandma while the tribe stands behind us gawking at all the people in the cavernous [*adj: resembling a large cave*] airport. To be honest, I want to gawk too, but I have to keep my attention at the task at hand – getting checked in for our flight to Istanbul!

"You will have two layovers," the pleasant lady says as she hands the tickets back to my grandma. "One in New York and one in Frankfurt."

"Germany!" I pipe up.

"Yes, that's right, Frankfurt, Germany," she says looking down at me. "But I'm sorry to say, you won't be able to leave the airport. You only have a two hour layover, and Frankfurt is a big airport."

I drop my new Pan Am bag to the floor in disappointment. It's a sturdy blue vinyl bag with a big white circle in the middle and the words Pan Am written across the middle of the circle. The circle has curved lines running across it, which I assume is trying to show it's round like the world. Since we're going halfway around the world, I think it's a very à *propos* [that's French for *appropriate*] symbol for an airline.

"It will take you some time to get to your gate for your final flight to Istanbul."

I put my bag back over my shoulder. That's right. I'm going to Istanbul. Exploring Frankfurt will have to wait for another day.

Finally we're ready to head to our gate. Gate is airport lingo for the place you go to get on your plane. It's not really a gate, it's a place that has lots of seats for people to wait until the flight attendant gets on a little speaker, like they use for ham radios, and tells everyone it's time to board the plane. Then she opens a glass door that lets you out on the runway where your plane is waiting. You go up some steps that they roll up to the side of the plane and step inside.

My family gets to wait with us. Well, kind of. Aaron is gabbing with one of the flight attendants at the little counter at our gate. Adam, Max, Peter, and Danny are running up and down the terminal trying to find planes that are coming in or taking off from the different gates.

It seems like forever before the flight attendant tells us we can board the plane.

My mother gets all sappy on me, of course.

"You behave yourself, Agnes," she says, buttoning the top button of my sweater set. She bought me a new robin-egg-blue one just for the trip – acrylic for easy wash and wear. Mom wasn't sure what kind of washing facilities we'd have. Grandma didn't know either. She also bought me a travel dictionary. Just when I think my mother is clueless, she goes and does something like that. I guess she knows me pretty well.

"Stay with your grandmother. No getting curious and wandering off by yourself."

Actually, she knows me *too* well.

"I won't," I say to reassure her, and I sincerely hope I'm right.

Mom sat down with me last night and told me how happy she is for me that I am going on this trip with Grandma. "I have never been farther than Fort Lauderdale," she told me. After Mom's dad died, Grandma Barb wanted to keep traveling to Florida to escape the Wisconsin winter, like she did when Grandpa Bill was still alive, so my mom would drive her down there and fly back so Grandma had a car to tool around in. Mom said this trip is a great opportunity, but I needed to keep my eyes open. "There are lots of good people in the world, Agnes, but there are some bad ones too."

I notice the line to get on the plane is getting short. "We gotta go, Mom."

My mom looks up and takes a deep breath. I don't think she's going to let that breath out until I come home again. I hope she doesn't pass out on the way back out to the car. She pulls me closer and squeezes all the air out of me. Aaron's still stuck to the check-in counter, but he manages to pull himself away to say goodbye.

"Have a great time, squirt." He rubs my head like he's the big man around the house. "Don't take any plugged nickels." I stare at him. That's just what dad would have said. (My dad told me this saying was started after someone cut a hole – or plug – out of the center of a coin, which made it not worth what it was supposed to be worth, in this case, a nickel.)

Grandma and I step outside and the wind tries to whip my skirt up around my ears. Now I know why Mom always insists I wear a slip! I don't need to be showing off my underwear to half the world. It's new too, but still.

I hear furious tapping on the big glass window at our gate. I turn and see Adam, Max, Peter, and Danny all waving frantically at me. I smile and wave back. You never know, I might die in a fiery plane crash and never see them again. I should make their memory of me at least a semi-pleasant one.

There is one flight attendant at the bottom of the steps smiling and repeating "Watch your step. Watch your step" so many times I'm guessing she says it in her sleep. The one standing just inside the plane has the same smile plastered on her face and her recording is "Welcome to Pan Am." They are all wearing a very crisp, sky-blue suit with a white blouse underneath. Their pill box hats sit on their perfectly coiffed hair [*coif* (I learned this word from Peggy): *to cut and arrange someone's hair*], and they all have on a lot of makeup and lipstick. Most of them are blond and have hair like Marilyn Monroe. Some are brunettes and look more like Elizabeth Taylor.

Another attendant helps us find our seats, helps Grandma stow her bag in the overhead compartment, and asks us if we want a pillow or blanket, then she moves on to the next person and repeats the whole process. I make a mental note so I can tell Peggy that if she wants to be a flight attendant, she needs to buy stock in the Maybelline makeup company, the Aqua Net hair spray company, and learn to lift heavy weights above her head.

Grandma lets me sit by the window so I get to see the luggage manhandled as they throw it from the luggage carts to the ramp that takes it up to the plane. I'm glad I didn't put anything that was real breakable in my bag. Once they close the door to the plane and we start to back out of our parking spot, the flight attendants stagger themselves along the aisle of the plane and demonstrate – in perfect unison – how to get buckled in; how, in case of an emergency, to use the oxygen mask that is above our heads and the life jacket that is tucked under our seat. As they are doing this, the flight attendant on the microphone at the front tells us what they are demonstrating. I bend down and confirm that the canary-yellow rubber thing each flight attendant is currently wearing around their necks is where it belongs. During the performance, the stewardesses (Grandma said that's another name for flight attendant) all move in unison so it's kind of fun to watch. I make another mental note for Peggy: learn group dances.

The takeoff is pretty smooth but my stomach feels like it takes a minute to catch up with the rest of me. Grandma Agee is reading her book as if it's just another trip to the market. Me, I'm plastered to the window watching the airport grow smaller every second, like someone is slowly dropping it out the window on a fishing line.

We take a slow turn, the plane tipping and banking to one side, and my stomach does its own maneuver. I have to sit back in my seat.

"Ya all right, Agnes?" Grandma Agee asks.

I just nod my head. I'm a little afraid if I open my mouth, something inside me is going to fly out.

"Would you like a cocktail or soda?"

I turn my head and there is the stewardess, standing behind a small metal cart that just fits in the aisle while another stewardess is pouring and handing soda in glasses to the people on the other side of the aisle.

"I'll have a rum and Coke," my grandmother says, then turns to me. "Agnes?"

"Do you have root beer?"

"I'm sorry, dear, we don't. We have juice, water, and Coke products."

"A Coke is fine," I say and think, *Tell Peggy to learn how to disappoint people but make it sound really nice.* My stewardess list is getting kind of long. I'm going to have to start writing things down in my notebook pretty soon.

With one hand she expertly puts down the tray that I didn't even notice was tucked in the seat in front of Grandma and sets down Grandma's drink along with a bag of peanuts with the other. I put down my own tray and she hands me an ice-filled glass of Coke, two bags of nuts, and with a wink and a polite smile, moves on to the next row of seats.

I enjoy my snack as I look out the window. I have to put my face up to the glass to see any details of the ground below us. It looks like what a map might look like if it was filled in with color – all the roads, rivers, and farm fields drawn with perfect accuracy. I grab my shoulder bag so I can pull out and study the maps I made of Turkey and Istanbul.

Then someone comes on the intercom, interrupting my thoughts.

"Good morning, ladies and gentleman, this is your captain speaking. It looks like we will have smooth sailing all the way to New York. We will be arriving at Idlewild Airport at approximately two fifteen Eastern time. The flight attendants will be serving you lunch as soon as you all receive your beverages, so sit back, relax, and enjoy your flight, and thank you for flying Pan Am."

As soon as he clicks off, I begin to smell our lunch, mixed with the acrid [*adj: bitter and unpleasant*] aroma of tobacco smoke. "I don't remember seeing a stove," I say to Grandma.

"They have precooked food that they heat up," Grandma explains.

And it is pretty good too. I get a refill of my soda with Grandma taking water this time. And just as the stewardess is about to put down our miniature food trays, the "smooth sailing" turns into "choppy seas" as the plane jostles everyone this way and that. The stewardess expertly balances the two trays she has in her hands like a juggler on the high wire. After a minute or so the plane finally settles down a little, enough for her to set them down in front of us. We automatically hold our trays in place so they don't land in our laps. We both get a warm ham and cheese sandwich on a small bakelite plate. It comes with a small serving of cooked carrots and a miniature brownie for dessert. Grandma and I both eat with one hand, holding our drinks in the other, trying to get our food to our mouths. It's like trying to eat while on a mini-rollercoaster. When I do manage to eat a bit of my food, I contemplate how to bring up the subject of my father and not have Grandma try and change the subject. All I can think about is what Uncle Bob said at the funeral dinner: "Not too surprising then that he got into…"

What was Uncle Bob going to say?! It was obviously something Grandma Agee didn't think I should know about, so it must not have been good. All kinds of things have been rolling around in my head. Did he get into…collecting knives? (I'd never seen them.) Did he get into…drinking martinis? (All I had ever seen my dad drink was a brandy when it was my parent's turn to have people over for card club.) Did he get into…trouble!? And if so, where and what kind? I am just dying to ask, but by her reaction to Uncle Bob, I know I can't ask her a direct question. It takes me all the way through to the brownie for me to figure out what to say.

I take one last sip of my now watered-down Coke, grasping the side of the glass with my teeth so it stays in place, and the captain comes back on telling us we have begun our descent (though my stomach has already figured that out) and that the stewardesses will be picking up our trays.

Drat. I lost my chance. But we have two more plane rides, so I still have time to find out what's up before we get to Istanbul and my mind gets pulled elsewhere. It doesn't take long and everything is stowed away, and we begin dropping even faster.

I desperately want to look out the window to see if I can spy the Brooklyn Bridge or the Empire State Building but I have to sit in my seat and keep my mouth shut again. The food in my stomach doesn't like the rapid change in altitude. I wasn't watching out the window so I'm surprised when we hit the ground and bounce a couple times until we're suddenly pushed forward, our seatbelts digging into our hips, as the plane brakes to a rapid roll. I look out the window and the plane turns so I can see the terminal and all the people scrambling around outside. The flight attendants are up and moving but they tell us to remain seated "until the plane has come to a complete stop." Once we stop, everyone, but Grandma and I, springs up and grabs the stuff out of the bins above their heads. I look at Grandma but she's looking in her compact and fixing her wine-colored lipstick, oblivious [*v: not aware of someone or something*] to everything going on around her.

"We can't get out until everyone in front of us moves forward, so we might as well wait here," she says without looking at me. Grandma seems to have that eyes-in-the-back-of-your head thing that my mother has in spades (an idiom Adam uses a lot that means *to have a lot of*). Grandma obviously has flown a ton of times, so she has to know what she's doing. I put the strap of my bag around my head and through one shoulder as my mother suggested – less likely to get snatched that way – and I wait patiently until people start to move.

An older gentleman behind us in the aisle waits for my grandma to stand, helps get our bags from above our heads, and lets us out before him. This happens a lot to Grandma on this trip. It's like she has a sign on her forehead that says "I'm old so could you help me, pretty please?"

The wind is mild when we step out of the plane and it's a bit cooler than it was back in Illinois.

We walk down the steps and into the busy airport terminal.

Grandma walks up to the nearest Pan Am counter. "Can you tell us what gate flight 346 is flying out of?"

The attendant looks on her clipboard. "Concourse E, Gate 14. Would you like a wheelchair, ma'am?"

"No, I'm perfectly able ta walk that far," Grandma says with a hint of indignation [*n: anger caused by something that is unfair or wrong*] in her voice.

The attendant plasters on a smile and tells us to have a good flight, though I'm guessing by the expression in her eyes she's really thinking something else entirely.

We look on the airport map and our gate is a ways away, but Grandma assures me we have plenty of time. We have an hour and a half layover. There are lots of small shops in the airport, just like in Chicago, and I spy a small bookstore. Grandma is walking kind of slow so I figure I have a few minutes to browse before she even suspects I'm not behind her. I wade into the bookstore and start scanning the shelves, wondering what new book I'll be able to read next. It's not that I buy newly released books or that I get them from the library; it usually takes the library a good month to get any of the newly published books in. It's because I have my own private book source. Well, the books aren't actually mine, they belong to Darlene Waynewright. She's a snooty girl at school who gets any book she wants, which usually means books on the bestseller list. And because I help Darlene in math class, she hands all her new books off to me, after she's read them, of course. It's a pretty good deal, really.

I see *To Kill a Mockingbird* on the display table and pick it up. Darlene has this one already and she said it's kind of spooky, so I open it up to see if I can tell what she's talking about. It's not until a man standing next to me accidentally drops a book on the floor that I notice I'm already on page fifteen. I look at my watch and realize I've been standing there reading for at least five minutes. I run out of the store and look down the crowded hallway, as if I could still see my grandmother somewhere in the distance. She is nowhere in sight.

Suddenly my throat goes dry and I can hardly swallow. My memory has gone blank. I can't remember the concourse (that's what airports call hallways) or the gate we're supposed to go to. I wasn't really paying attention when the stewardess told us since I figured Grandma Agee had it all under control. *Great! I promised my mom I wouldn't wander off and now look what I've done. I'm not even out of the United States and I'm already lost.* I close my eyes and try and concentrate. *I think it was concourse E – E for Agee,* I say to myself, picturing the map of the airport in my mind. *But I don't remember the gate number. I think it had two numbers and an f in it some-where: Gate fifteen? Gate fifty-three? Gate forty-five?* I sigh. Nothing is appearing on the underside of my eyelids. This is the only chance I'll ever have in my whole life to visit an exotic place like Istanbul and I've blown it. I'm guessing Grandma's already on the plane and they're on the runway ready to take off. She has asked them to wait for me, of course, but they tell her they can't delay the plane any longer.

I sigh again as I drop my head and open my eyes. And there, right in front of my white Ked sneakers is a pair of familiar looking tan pumps. Attached to the pumps is a familiar A-line skirt and matching jacket. The person in the jacket has her elbows jutting out to the side because the lady has her hands on her hips. I know who these items belong to, of course, but I can't seem to make myself look up into her face.

"I'm sorry," I say, looking back down at Grandma Agee's shoes. "Did we miss our plane?"

"If ya wanted somethin' to read, ya could have just asked," my grandmother says.

What did she say?

I look down at my hands and realize I'm still holding a copy of *To Kill a Mockingbird*. I look up at Grandma Agee to explain but she has already stepped into the bookstore. She is at the counter, pointing to the book I'm holding and pulling out her wallet.

I run up next to her, about to say that it isn't necessary to buy me the book when the clerk hands my grandmother her receipt, a package of breath mints, and a roll of Lifesavers. Grandma hands me the Lifesavers and directs me out of the bookstore with a little shove.

"Thanks, Grandma," I say as we make our way down the corridor, this time at a considerably faster pace. I could explain to her that I've got two other books along with me – one in my Pan Am bag and one in my suitcase, but she doesn't seem upset with me for getting lost, and if I've ever learned anything in my twelve years on this planet, it is to never turn down a free book.

We make it to our gate with just five minutes to spare, and most of the passengers have already boarded the plane. There are different looking people at this gate compared to the Midwesterners who were lined up in Chicago. I can tell these people are from different countries by the color of their skin and the luggage they are carrying.

Luggage!

"Grandma! Where is our luggage?"

"They will transfer it from our Chicago flight ta this one," she said with nary a [*adj: not a single*] tremor in her voice. (I heard the word nary in an old movie once and I like to use it when I can.)

I take a deep breath and have to tell myself to believe her again. Grandma hasn't been wrong yet.

The same cookie-cutter flight attendants are here as in Chicago, they only vary slightly in height and hair color. This plane is bigger, three seats on each side instead of two, but we go through the same takeoff procedures, so I'm ready for my drink and snack and can't wait to see what's on the menu for dinner. That little bookstore fiasco has given me an appetite and even though I've chewed my way through half of the Lifesavers already, they just aren't doing the trick. I completely forget about the burning question about my dad as I watch the skyline of Manhattan Island and Lady Liberty shrink away from us, quickly replaced by ripples of blue water as far as I can see.

A

The man behind me pushes his tray up against the back of my seat and I'm woken from my sleep. Reluctantly I pull my head out of a most interesting dream where I'm lost in the desert and I'm trying to find my grandmother. I didn't even realize I had fallen asleep. I pull my head off a pillow that is propped on Grandma's shoulder and a string of spit follows me. I wipe my mouth and look at Grandma to see if she's seen what I've done. She's looking at a picture of a small boy that looks a lot like my brother Adam, but I'm not sure why Grandma Agee would be looking at a picture of Adam. I spy *To Kill a Mockingbird* tucked in the kangaroo-type pouch on the back of the seat in front of me, bookmark in place. Grandma must have put it there when I fell asleep. She also must have been the one to give me the pillow that was under my head and the blanket that is covering me. My stomach tells me we're descending again. Then, without warning, the bottom falls out of the plane.

Chapter 3

Well, it doesn't really fall out, it just feels that way. We're experiencing what the pilot now tells us over the intercom is turbulence [*n: moving in an irregular or violent way*]. I look outside and the blue sky I saw as I was eating my chicken and mashed potatoes hours earlier is now full of black and angry clouds. I can see flashes of lightning in the inky blackness, like someone is trying to light a lighter that just won't catch. And to add to the tense situation, I can see the wings of the airplane waving up and down unnaturally as if they're doing their part to keep the plane in the air.

We're descending again, but this time a lot faster than we did on our last flight. I press myself back into my seat, grasp my dad's St. Christopher medal, and say a silent prayer that the wings don't snap off as we dip and turn our way down through the clouds. I thought our ride to New York was bumpy but this feels like Danny has a hold of us and is running through the house dipping us under chair legs and rolling us around sharp corners. I admonish [*v: to speak to someone in a way that expresses disapproval or criticism*] myself for not checking out the plane's aerodynamic capacity before I set foot inside it. The wing to cabin ratio just doesn't appear to be sustainable [*adj: able to be used without being destroyed*], at least in the middle of an angry storm cloud.

Amid the cigarette-smoke-filled cabin, my nose catches a whiff of an unmistakable smell and my stomach decides it's finally had enough. Before I know what's happening, I add my own gastric perfume to the mix by puking my dinner into a small paper bag my observant grandmother just put in front of me. Grandma hands the bag to a seemingly unruffled stewardess, who then gives my grandmother a moist washcloth. Grandma Agee wipes my mouth then folds the washcloth and places it on my forehead. I don't really notice because I'm concentrating very hard on not throwing-up again. We've dropped far enough out of the clouds that the plane has leveled off and we make our final drop into the Frankfurt airport as if nothing has even happened.

A

As I walk off the plane, I still feel like I had one too many rides on the Tilt-O-Whirl after eating a chili-cheese dog and Grandma Agee can tell. Without saying a thing, she grasps my hand and we walk directly to our next gate, where she sits me down in a chair so she can find me a soda to sip on – the same remedy my mother uses for an upset stomach. The rest of the trip is a blur because once we're in the air, I easily fall asleep, even though it's early in the morning and they're serving scrambled eggs and bacon, my favorite breakfast. My stomach tightens at the greasy smell as they pass out the trays, and Grandma hands me my damp washcloth, instructing me to put it over my mouth and nose and to just breathe out of my mouth. It helps enough that I start to doze, though I realize I'm losing my last chance to ask my grandma what kind of bad thing my father had gotten into. My stomach doesn't care, and at that moment, neither do I.

A

I'm jolted awake as we land at Turkey's Ataturk International Airport. My mouth feels like I've eaten one of my brother's used socks, but my stomach seems to have gone back into hiding so I feel better overall. Plus we're in Istanbul, Turkey! What's there to complain about?

Well, we're not actually in Istanbul yet, as I was soon to find out. We are quite a ways outside of the city, and it takes us a very long and stinky bus ride on a very iffy bus to get to our hotel. The thing coughs and sputters so much I think it has a cold. The ride is smelly not only because of the smoke the bus spews every time it belches, but from all the people that we pick up along the way. By the end of the trip there is a man standing in the aisle holding a live chicken as if he has just gone to the corner store to pick up dinner; there is a crying child just in front of us, who obviously doesn't like his full diaper any more than we do; and the driver has to shift to a lower gear just to get the full bus up even the smallest hill. The bus is so packed, in fact, that by the time we make our hundredth stop – yes, I'm exaggerating, but not by much – the driver has to leave the door open so the last man on the bus can hang halfway out the door. As Dorothy in "The Wizard of Oz" once said, "Toto, we're not in Kansas anymore."

But it's all worth it once we step through the doors of our hotel: the Hotel Zanzibar. We're greeted by a smiling, lightly-tanned-looking man in a suit and tie. He actually doesn't have a tan; it's just what the people of Turkey look like. I'm envious, really. Being of Irish-German descent (meaning my parents and grandparents were from Ireland and Germany), each summer it takes me a couple good burns to get my skin to the color these people wake up to every day.

The man in the tie has gone behind the tall desk and found Grandma Agee's reservation. With a scowl, a snap of his finger, and a quick flick of his wrist, he directs a young boy in a crisp navy-blue uniform and pill hat to immediately take our luggage, like we had been waiting an hour for him to show up and actually it had been less than three minutes. He's no bigger than Max so he can't be over ten, but he doesn't seem to notice the man's scowl because he smiles at us as if we are his long lost cousins.

"Room 502," the man in the suit says. The young boy grabs every bag we let him carry, says, "Please follow me," and walks briskly to the elevator. I feel like the Queen of Sheba until I look closely at the poor kid as we all stand in the elevator, waiting for it to creak its way up to the fifth floor. He is sweating like a pig, as Adam would say, and he smells a little like he's been in a barnyard, too. I'm not sure where Adam got that sweating pig idea. Pigs don't sweat. My brother Peter, who wants to be farmer and actually helps my Uncle Roger on his farm, says pigs stay cool by wallowing in the mud. So really pigs have a bad rap for being dirty. They are actually kind of smart; if they cover themselves in wet mud, it evaporates off their skin like water but even slower and so it keeps them cool.

It is mid-afternoon, so I guess the boy has been in that hot monkey suit most of the day. I had taken my sweater off a while ago because of the heat, so I am sure he is really cooking. I'm pleased when Grandma takes a dollar out of her purse and pushes it in his hand before he leaves us in our sunny room. I notice his nametag says "Baris." I make a mental note to remember that the next time we meet.

"I'm going ta take a short rest before dinner, Agnes. You're welcome ta look about, but please don't leave the hotel," she says as she slips off her pumps and stretches out on the bed.

If Grandma hadn't already closed her eyes, I wouldn't have known what to say. No adult has ever let me "look about" unsupervised. Never! I chalk this up to Granny not really having been around me too much. I have a reputation for getting into scrapes because I wasn't paying attention; at least that's what my parents always say. It actually isn't that I don't pay attention, I am just not paying attention to the things they think I should. In fact, I am usually paying too close attention to something else, usually something much more interesting, at least to me. But after the incident in the airport, I had promised myself that I wouldn't get into trouble again on this trip. I think I owe Grandma that much, since she picked *me* to go along with her and not one of my brothers. I only hope that circumstances will work with me on this, unlike what usually happens.

Our room is longer than it is wide with two neatly-made twin beds side by side; a small bathroom just big enough for a one-person shower, a sink, and a toilet; a chair next to each bed; a closet only big enough for a few day's-worth of clothes and a small dresser. My first place to explore is the small balcony outside of the glass sliding doors.

I slide the door open and Granny lifts her head on account of all the noises that flood into the room. "Sorry," I whisper and quickly close the door behind me.

Our balcony looks out on the street we drove in on and is filled with trucks, cars, and people going this way and that. I've never seen such a busy place, even in LaCrosse, the closest large city to De Soto. LaCrosse has a population of only 47,000. Istanbul's population is closer to 1.3 million and that was five years ago when the encyclopedia Peggy was reading out of had been published. The Hotel Zanzibar sits on the side of a slope that leads down to what looks like a river but is actually an inlet [*n: a narrow area of water that goes into the land from a sea or lake*] of the Bosporus. The Bosporus is considered a strait because it connects the Black Sea (one very big lake) in the north with the Sea of Marmara (another very big lake) in the south. The inlet is called the Golden Horn because it's supposed to be shaped like a horn and it's considered "Golden" because of all the riches of the area. The inlet is just as busy as the street, with motor boats and large sail boats tied up to docks or moving up and down the waterway. Across the Golden Horn there is another small rise that is covered with three, four, and five story buildings and has at its peak, a round brick tower. Everything is painted in a gold light as the sun makes its way to the western horizon. I have to squint and shade my eyes to look west, but I can tell it's also filled with buildings as far as I can see.

I look down to the street again and notice an area right next to the hotel entrance where people are sitting at cloth-covered tables. And as I stretch to get a better look, my best hair pin, the one with the glittering bumble bee on it that my grandma Barb gave me, falls out of my hair and drops five stories down onto a table where two people are sitting eating. Here I am, just standing and things have already started to conspire to get me into trouble. But it can't be helped. I'm not going to leave the hairpin my dead grandmother gave me in Istanbul. And the sidewalk isn't really off the hotel's grounds; not really.

As fast as I can, I open and close the sliding door, but Grandma Agee is quietly snoring away and doesn't hear me. I leave the room and find the stair-well so I don't have to waste time waiting for the maddeningly-slow elevator. Once down in the lobby, I see a set of open double doors to what is obviously the hotel's restaurant; it's filled with the same round, cloth-covered tables that are out on the sidewalk.

I step inside and a very pretty lady in a tight black skirt and white blouse steps up to me with an arm full of large menus. I know they're menus because there are people at some of the table look-ing at them.

"May I help you," she asks in English and in a way that tells me a young girl probably shouldn't be here without an adult. I have to think fast.

"I'm looking for my parents. I fell asleep and they left me a note saying they would be down here." I knew if I was vague [*adj: not clear in meaning*] enough about my answer, it would leave me more wiggle room when I ended up not finding my parents since, of course, they weren't really there. I look around as if I'm trying to find them.

"I don't see them," I say and start to blink fast, as if I'm going to start crying. Adults hate to see a kid in distress, especially a girl. I pretend to just now see the doors that lead to the sidewalk tables. "May I please look outside? Maybe they're sitting there enjoying the nice evening in your beautiful city," I say, then immediately cringe inwardly. I asked permission, like grownups always like, but I might have laid it on a bit thick adding the "beautiful city" comment.

The lady doesn't seem to notice, however, and motions me to the open doors. "But of course," she says with a smile.

I step through the doors and start looking around, in case the lady is watching me, but I turn to look back and she's busy walking a family of four to a table.

I take a deep breath and relax, changing my focus to finding the table my pin dropped onto. From above I had noticed two sets of four tables running along the sidewalk. I know that the pin dropped onto the third table from the main steps into the lobby and it was a table closest to the building. I'm glad to see that the two people sitting at that table are an older couple. Older people are more likely to have grandchildren, so they are more likely to be nice to a young girl like me.

I inch a bit closer to see if I can spy my pin, but it is nowhere to be seen. I still have my bag over my shoulder, so I take it off, open it up as if I am looking for something, and make like I accidentally drop it on the ground, aiming the opening toward the second table in. There is a single man sitting at the second table, and in what sounds like French, he starts talking to me as he helps me pick up the items that have spilled out or, more accurately, that I have thrown out.

I kneel down and take the things from him, thanking him and smiling my widest smile, in case he doesn't understand English. But what I really want to do is scream and tell him to stop already. This wasn't the plan. I have to fumble with a few things and let them drop again. This allows me to get on my hands and knees and look under the third table for my pin. But still no luck. The floor is as clean as a whistle.

I'm not sure how a whistle is supposed to be clean when it's probably full of someone's spit, but it's another idiom I looked up in the idiom book at the library because my dad always says that one...I mean he USED TO say that one. I still can't get used to him not being here.

After I stand and the man helps me brush the invisible dirt from my skirt, I back away from him in the direction of the elderly couple, nodding, smiling, and throwing thank yous at him as fast as they will come.

The older couple has been watching the whole incident, of course, and they are still looking at me. I have to think fast again for some way to more closer to examine their table without appearing as if I'm a street urchin looking for a handout. [BTW: By The Way, the term "street urchin" has nothing to do with the sea creature that is covered in spines and lives on the floor of the ocean; it's a term my grandma Barb use to use for kids that are always hanging out on the street, who she thought were looking for trouble. I know the kids she was referring to in De Soto and mostly they were just bored and looking for something to do.]

Then without warning, said urchin rides by on a rusty, old bike and at the very last table, he does the most extraordinary thing: he nabs a basket of rolls right off the table without hardly slowing down. I can tell this kid works the streets because his clothes are no cleaner than his bike and his hair has not seen a comb in days, make that weeks! The people at the table yell at him, of course, and so does the waiter, once he figures out what's just happened. So everyone, including the old couple, have turned to watch the festivities and I get my chance.

I scan the table and there is my pin, sticking halfway out of the ladies cream pie. With no time to lose, I stick my finger in the pie and flip my bee pin high into the air. The woman notices the movement but turns around slow enough that all she sees me do is catch the pin in my hand. I toss it up and catch it again a few more times, as if I have been standing here doing that the whole time. I watch the boy on the bike drop the rolls down his shirt and toss the basket high enough in the air that the waiter, who has almost caught up to him now, catches it before it hits the ground. Everyone applauds and I give up a two-fingered whistle that Adam would be proud of. The boy doesn't turn around but waves his hand in appreciation.

A

Grandma and I end up eating dinner at the hotel restaurant because Grandma slept longer than she wanted to so she wants to eat somewhere close by, despite my hints at wanting to try someplace more..."Turkish." I'm sure this is a fine Turkish restaurant, but I don't want to cross paths with the restaurant hostess again. And in fact, she does look at me strangely when I walk back in with my grandmother instead of my long lost parents. I quickly explain that my grandmother really wanted to try their food after I told her how good it smelled, so I agreed to go with her, since my family "is not here." *Yeah, like on a different continent!* But, of course, I don't tell her that.

Back in the room after dinner, I pull out the small notebook I put in my bag and write down the Turkish sentences I have in my composition notebook. I brought along the small notepad so I can write down important things that I happen upon. I also use it to write down things like these Turkish words so I can get at them easily. My composition notebook usually has all my important information, but it's just too big to take with me as we travel around town. I got the sentences out of the *Travel Guide to Turkey* that I took out of the library before I left. I write down *Merhaba* (**mer**-*ha-ba* – Hello); *Ingilizce* *biliyor musunuz?* (*een-gee-**leez**-jeh bee-**lee**-yor moo-soo-nooz?* – Do you speak English?); *Anlamıyorum* (*an-**la**-muh-yo-room* – I don't understand); and most important: *Nerede banyo?* (**neh**-reh-deh bann-yo?* –Where is the bathroom?). Grandma told me at dinner that tomorrow we're going to go sightseeing, so I want to be prepared.

I'm pretty excited so it's hard for me to fall asleep. Since Grandma is already snoozing away, I pull out my flashlight, drop down off the side of my bed – away from Grandma – and pull out the paperback copy of the *Arabian Nights* that Peggy gave me as a going away gift. I kind of want to find out what happens to Jem Finch and Boo Radley in *To Kill a Mockingbird*, but I figure I'm in a foreign country now, I should read something that wasn't written in the United States.

The prologue in the *Arabian Nights* book tells me all the different stories in the book are really old, like from the 14th century, which actually means the 1300s. I'm not sure why the century is always a number higher than the year, but that's how it's done, I swear.

The people who wrote the prologue don't really seem to know where the stories came from, but they think they first started in India or Persia. The book says that some of the later stories were probably written by Antonie Galland, a Frenchman who translated the books when he was living in Istanbul in 1701. How cool is that! A book that you can buy in the USA in 1961 was translated in Istanbul in 1701. I have a feeling I'll see a lot of that kind of thing while I'm here.

I don't know if you're familiar with the *Arabian Nights*, or *The Thousand and One Nights* as it was originally called, but the whole idea of the stories is that this king, King Shahryar, liked to marry a lot, but for some reason, he would kill his wife the day after they got hitched. (Nice guy, huh?) Well, he finally marries a woman by the name of Scheherazade who is a bit smarter than the old king. Every night she starts telling him a story, but she doesn't tell him the next part of the story until the next night so that she gets to live another day. She does this for so long that eventually they have a son, so the king decides he isn't going to kill her after all. Smart girl that Scheherazade!

I start with *Ali Baba and the Forty Thieves* and I get into the story so much, I lose track of time. That happens to you too, right? Your mom or dad tells you to pick up your room and as you pick your books off the floor, you see the book *Treasure Island* and you remember you left off just when Jim Hawkins had found the treasure map. You start reading again and before you know it, it's an hour later and your mother is calling you to dinner. You throw your dirty clothes and candy wrappers into your closet, toss the bedspread over the unmade bed, and voila, the room's clean! – mostly anyway.

"Agnes, where are ya?"

I turn to see the dark figure of my grandmother standing by the side of her bed. I see by the glow-in-the-dark arms of the alarm clock on the nightstand between our beds that it's 12:15 A.M.! I turn off my flashlight and slide into bed. "I was just going to bed."

"I should say so," she says and heads off to the bathroom.

I am so tired I barely hear the flush of the toilet before I drift off to never land.

Chapter 4

Standing outside on the sidewalk, the sun is bright but it is early so it's not too hot yet. We're both in colorful summer dresses and sweaters, ready to take in the sights and sounds of this exotic [*adj: very different, strange or unusual*] city. I tell Grandma Agee that the temperature only gets up to the sixties in late May in Turkey so we shouldn't need to worry. At least that's what the travel guidebook said. Plus I can tell that we're not too far from a lot of water; the air feels like it does when I'm fishing with my dad on the Mississippi. I look at my grandma and sigh. *I guess I won't be fishing with my dad anymore.*

The same gentleman that greeted us yesterday – he told us to call him Vasil – is standing half in the street and half on the sidewalk, trying to wave down a taxi. I explained to Grandma that the Top-kapi Palace (pronounced kind of like: *toep-cop-u*), the Hagia Sophia (*hi-ya so-fee-ya*), and Sultanahmet Mosque (*sul-tan-a-met maask*) are all right next to each other, so that would be the logical place to start. Vasil agrees with my choice, but says we can't miss the Grand Bazaar on the way back to the hotel. "It is like nothing you have ever seen before," he assures us.

I can't wait!

Vasil finally gets us a taxi and he tells the driver where we would like to go. He ushers us into the car warning us, "Be so kind as to hold tight to your purses, ladies," he says, almost like he is embarrassed. "I am sorry to say, there are people who prey on the tourists, even beautiful ones such as yourselves," he says as he touches me under the chin. I probably turn a hundred shades of pink and remind myself to look up *thank you* in Turkish when I get back to our room.

The ride to our destination is certainly an interesting one. The driver bobs and weaves through the traffic like Grandma is dying and he has to get us to the hospital before she croaks, until Grandma smacks the driver on the shoulder and yells at him to slow down. He must understand English because he immediately drives at a more normal pace. Now I can gawk at the street vendors and all the people dressed for work who are walking on the sidewalks along our way. It seems like it could be any big city in the states, though most people here have dark hair and are darker-skinned than in Wisconsin. When we step out of the cab and see the two-story, walled courtyard and six towering minarets of the Sultanahmet, or Blue Mosque, in front of us, all I can do is stare.

Vasil has already told us what the taxi ride should cost, "Forty-five lira, no more. This is tip, also. It is fine. He knows!" Vasil said emphatically, pointing to the driver. I know that sounds like a lot of money, but Grandma explained to me that one dollar is equal to nine lira so forty-five lira is five dollars. Grandma hands the man forty-five lira, even though he has obviously asked for a different amount. Grandma shakes her head and tells him, "No, no" as she shoves me out of the cab. I'm sure glad Grandma is with me. I'd have given the man whatever he had asked for. He seemed pretty insistent.

The minute we step toward the mosque we are surrounded by a passel [*n: a large number of people or things*] of small boys with scarves draped over each arm that make them look like small colorful birds. A few industrious ones are wearing a scarf on their head, as well. They all step back and audibly sigh as Grandma Agee slowly pulls a soft-green scarf out of her bag as if she's a magician pulling a rabbit out of a hat. The boys fall back and quickly swarm around the next female to step up to the entrance without something on her head.

I lean toward my grandmother. "I forgot my scarf," I whisper. I actually knew that women needed to cover their heads in a mosque (I had read it in a book, of course), but in my haste to make it down to breakfast on time (I was a bit tired from staying up so late reading), I forgot it.

Grandma doesn't skip a beat; she reaches in her purse for her wallet, gives me three ten-lira bills, and points to the swarm of boys. I pull out my notepad and check the translation for hello. I figure I'll start with something simple and try other words if I run into a snag. I tentatively step up to one of the boys on the edge of the pack and tap him on the shoulder.

"*Merhaba*," I say and give him a slight nod.

He is one of the boys who has a scarf on his head, a rather pretty pastel blue one.

"*Merhaba*," he replies and grins.

He instantly unfurls his wings from in front of him and smiles when I hold out my money. He gives me his undivided attention, trying to steer me to this scarf or that one. I don't see anything I like, and I eventually point to the one on his head. He points to his head and nods in agreement. I start to reach for the scarf but he frowns deeply and shakes me off, then he runs up to a friend not far away. He is talking a mile a minute and I can't understand a word he is saying, of course. He points to me, to the scarf on his head, and then starts to rummage among the scarves that line the other boy's arms. He finally finds his prize and runs back to me with a wide grin and the pale blue scarf flowing wildly above his head. He bows and ceremoniously hands me the scarf.

I instantly wish I had looked up how to ask the cost of something in Turkish but I didn't think of it so I try in English. "How much?" I ask him, showing him my lira bills.

He holds up two fingers then seven. "Twenty-seven," he says in perfectly good English.

I hand him the money, and he reaches in his pocket for the change.

"Keep the change," I say as I shake my head and start walking away. I keep watching him to make sure he understands and he waves and grins wide. "Keep the change" is something he probably learned pretty quickly in his business.

"Was there any change?" Grandma asks.

"Not much, so I just gave him a tip," I say with a smile. I figure if Grandma Agee did it, so should I. Grandma nods her head but gives me a funny look. I suppose I should have asked since it was her money I was giving away. I make a mental note to ask the next time the situation arises.

We enter the building on the edge of the large, closed-in courtyard, close to the entrance to the mosque itself. I step back to get a better look at the building, and I suddenly understand how the ants in our driveway must feel, seeing the red-roofed domes of the mosque loom story upon story above us. The huge-O main dome sits on top of the mosque and the semidomes of the mosque (which is an apt [*adj: appropriate or suitable*] name because they are like full domes but just cut in half) are like stepping stones leading up to it. *It must have taken a kajillion slaves to make this thing,* I think as we step up to a man in a tan robe with what Grandma told me is a fez on his head – kind of a tall pill box hat.

"Tours this way," he says in English as good as

the boy with the scarves. I guess they get a lot of people visiting who speak English to practice on.

A

We spend half the morning on a guided tour of the mosque with people from Germany; we are the only Americans in our group so Sheikh, our guide, speaks German during the tour with a smattering of English when he notices we look particularly confused. I mention this to Grandma Agee after our tour is done and the only thing she says is, "Welcome to the world of the minority." It's a world I've never lived in before and I understand why people don't like it; it makes you feel insignificant and kind of on the outside of things.

I hadn't read up much on this mosque before I left, but Sheikh tells us it was built by Sultan Ahmet The First in the early 17th century, which is actually 1600 something, if you remember how that works.

This building is like no other building I have ever been in. First of all, they make you take off your shoes and it's not like it was at Grandma Barb's house when she got new carpet in her living room; she made you take off your shoes so you wouldn't track dirt on her nice, new rug. You take off your shoes in a mosque because it is considered a holy place, like when Moses took off his sandals when he heard God talking to him from the burning bush. (See Miss Mueller, I did pay attention in Sunday school.) Though, my guess is that churches started out like Grandma Barb's house, too. People were mostly farmers way back when, and just like at my house, when Peter comes back from working on Uncle Roger's farm, we really don't want the stuff and the smell he has on his boots in the house. And the ladies who cleaned the churches way back when (and it we all know it was the ladies who did the cleaning) didn't want that in their clean churches either. But that's just my theory [n: *an idea or set of ideas that is intended to explain facts or events*]. Anyway, I'm digressing.

They call this place the Blue Mosque for a good reason; there are beautiful blue-colored tiles all around what Sheikh told us is the prayer hall – the large square room below all those domes, where everyone comes to pray. The prayer hall takes up most of the whole mosque, just like a church nave [n: *the long center part of a church where people sit*] takes up most of a church. But there are no benches to sit on in this building and later I find out why. Sheikh says the tiles were made not far from Istanbul in the city of Iznik. But get this, Iznik used to be called Nicea (*ni-see-a*). Sound familiar to any of you Catholics out there? It took me a while but I finally put two and two together (another idiom, if you hadn't noticed, which means *to figure something out using the information available*). Iznik or Nicea was where they wrote the Catholic Nicene Creed. Something I say every day in church was thought up just miles from where I am standing! I'm sure happy Grandma Agnes brought me along to Turkey. It is the coolest place!

But back to the mosque. The tiles in the Blue Mosque are not just blue. If you walk up close, you can see lots of red flowers and green leaves mixed in with the various shades of blue. Apparently, tiles were what all the best mosques of that time had used so, of course, that is what Sultan Ahmet The First wanted for his mosque. I don't know if the sultan was trying to impress God or his taxpayers, but whoever it was, I can say that this place gets a big thumbs up! I could spend hours just gazing up at the colorful domes. They look like the kaleidoscope that my brother Aaron has but much better, even though the domes don't turn. I get lost in what I'm looking at so many times during our tour that Grandma has to keep hold of my sweater so I don't get left behind. There is just too much to see.

The Hagia Sophia, or *Aya Sofya* as they say in Turkey, is next on our tour and it is only about three blocks away, so it doesn't take long to walk there. It is bigger than the Blue Mosque, and it's sitting on a small rise, so that makes it seem even larger. They build churches on hills in Wisconsin, too and probably for the same reason.

As we get closer, I can tell the Hagia Sophia is older than the Blue Mosque; the construction is different and it looks like it's crumbling in places. We pay our entrance fee, put on our scarves, (just in case) and step inside. This mosque is no longer open as a church so we have the freedom to roam almost everywhere on the main floor. It's eleven thirty and there are no more tours until the afternoon, so we just look around ourselves. We head right for the prayer hall with the rest of the tourists and for good reason.

What hits you first thing is the size of the place. It even puts the Blue Mosque to shame. I thought I was an ant when I stood in front of the Blue Mosque. Now, standing inside this huge room, I feel like a flea. The inside is not in as good a shape as the Blue Mosque, and I find out why by standing with my back to a tour that is partway done. Grandma Agee notices what I'm doing and stealthily [*adj: quietly and secretly in order to avoid being noticed*] slides up next to me as I pretend to look at something on the wall in front of me. The guide tells everyone that the building is 1400 years old and is fifty-six meters, or 184 feet high. (They use centimeters and meters here like our science teacher, Mr. Pearson, says they do most everywhere but in the US. Kind of odd that we've stuck with the imperial system of measurement – inches and feet – but there it is, as Mr. M. would say.) I check the notes I took during our tour of the Blue Mosque; that's fifteen meters (or about sixteen and a half feet) higher than the Blue Mosque. It's hard to imagine back 1400 years. And how did they manage to construct a building that could last this long? I am impressed, again!

Grandma turns and follows the tour group when they start to move, so I step right up next to her, facing the guide like we're part of the group. He is talking about the eight round, really big signs that are hanging all around the top of the prayer hall, just below the domes. "These medallions were put up after the mosque was converted from a Greek Orthodox Christian church to an Islamic mosque," the guide says.

This makes sense because the figures on the different medallions look like the Arabic writing that is on the back of the door in our hotel room. Don't worry, I'm not such a brainiac that I know Latin *and* Arabic. I only know it's Arabic because Grandma Agee told me it was.

"The writing on the medallions are names of important people in the Islamic religion such as Allah, or God in Islam," he says and points to a sign on the left, "and Muhammad, a prophet," he says, motioning right. "When they converted this building to a mosque, they covered many of the Christian mosaics [*n: decorations made of small pieces of colored glass*]. If you follow me, I will show you one of these mosaics."

We walk to the southeast entrance and see a mosaic on a small section of wall just above the doors. "In the center there is a depiction of Mary holding her young son, Jesus, and the men in robes on each side of her are past Turkish emperors."

I notice all four of the figures have a halo-like thing around their heads, which is a not so subtle [*adj: hard to notice or see, indirect*] hint that these people are really important or really holy in the Christian pecking order of things. (If you didn't know, someone came up with the term "pecking order" by watching chickens. In a flock of chickens, there is always one chicken that is the dominant [*adj: more important, powerful, or successful than most or all others*] chicken. This chicken will peck other chickens without getting pecked back. "Top dog" is like pecking order, because in a pack of dogs, there is always a dominant dog or "top dog.")

Our tour is interrupted only briefly by a haunting chant that is piped through the building with speakers and seems to surround us. The guide says it is the call to prayer and happens five times each day. We're almost done with our tour when this happens and when we step outside, the courtyard is filling up with all manner of people, mostly men from what I can tell, with little rugs tucked under their arms. I watch as each one in turn, unrolls the rug right behind the man in front of him or beside him in the open space and kneels down and starts to pray, tipping forward to touch his forehead to the ground. Now I know why mosques don't have pews. I can't help but wonder if that's where the idea of Aladdin and his carpet came from, though from my memory of the Aladdin story, I don't think he went to a mosque on a regular basis. I'll have to check the original Aladdin story in my *Arabian*

Nights book to see if it's any different than the version I read as a kid.

Grandma and I are both kind of hungry so we look around for some place to eat. We smell it before we see it. There is a smoky, spicy aroma in the air and it makes my stomach growl.

"I smell something good," I say.

"It does smell good," Grandma agrees.

We walk out of the complex of buildings that surround the mosque and head to the street, following our noses like Elmer Fudd does in a Bugs Bunny cartoon. Across the street there is a row of small food carts. As I step up onto the curb, a boy bumps into me so hard he almost knocks me over. He grabs for my arm and holds on tight so I don't fall.

"So sorry. So sorry," he says with a heavy Turkish accent as he pulls his other hand out of his pocket and starts brushing me off like I *had* fallen down or something. "You okay. No harm done." He finally stops talking and actually looks me in the face and he just stares at me, as if he's never seen a girl from America before. Then a slight grin creeps across his lips.

The boy looks a little older than me and is wearing beat-up shoes, very worn jeans, and a dirty t-shirt that has a picture of John Wayne wearing a cowboy hat on the front. The boy has eyes the color of warm cocoa, teeth as white as the lady in the Pepsodent toothpaste ad, and hair that sticks up all over the place, and for some odd reason, I think I've seen him before.

My cheeks go red from his stare and it takes me a while to reply. "I'm okay," I say. "Yes, no harm done."

Grandma Agee is standing over us now, scowling at the boy, so he gives us both a pleasant smile, a two-finger salute, and he walks over to pick up his rusty, old bike. It isn't until he starts walking away that I recognize him.

It's the kid who took the basket off the table outside of our hotel! I'd recognize that wild head of hair anywhere! I feel like flagging him down, but what am I going to say? *Hey, I know you. You're the kid who stole those buns.* It sounds kind of dumb in my head, so I decide it will sound even dumber coming out of my mouth, so I just turn with Grandma Agee and head for a food cart.

We pick out what the sign says is *lahmacun*: a round piece of cooked dough with a glob of some wonderful smelling meat, something white smeared on it, and some greens that look like lettuce out of our garden only darker in color. We find a free bench to sit down to eat. I set my bag on the ground at my feet and put my sandwich on my lap. Gazing down at the *lahmacun*, I wonder how best to get it in my mouth. I have never eaten anything like this before. I look at the food cart where we bought our sandwich from and there is a man handing a little girl, who looks to be about eight, one of these sandwiches. She immediately folds it in half and takes a bite. The man, who is probably her dad, directs her to a bench right next to ours. My throat gets tight, and I kind of lose my appetite. I look over at Grandma Agee and I suddenly remember the question I have for her about my dad.

"Grandma?"

Grandma Agee looks at me with her mouth full. She doesn't seem to have any trouble knowing how to eat the sandwich.

"Uncle Bob said something at the funeral that I was wondering about," I say.

Grandma finishes chewing and dabs her mouth with the back of her hand. "Sure, sweetheart. What do you want to know?"

I look into my Grandmother's face, not sure if she's going to get upset with me like she did Uncle

Bob, but right now, I have a strong urge to find out what he was going to say.

"Well...you might not like this...You seemed to get upset when he said it."

Grandma Agee looks puzzled, as if she's trying to remember what I'm talking about but can't.

"Uncle Bob and I were talking about books...he said that my dad liked books about spies and detectives (I looked up the authors after he had mentioned them at the funeral) and that it wasn't surprising then that he got into..."

And before I can finish, a young boy runs past us quicker than Flash Gordon, taking my bag right along with him.

Chapter 5

It takes me a few seconds to realize what has just happened but when I do, I immediately stand up, which means my sandwich falls on the ground. Grandma Agee is already standing, looking down the sidewalk after the boy. I jump over my *lahmacun* and start running after the kid.

"Agnes!" Grandma yells, running after me. "Come back here!"

I can still see him, my bag now over his head and shoulder so he can run faster, so I really don't want to slow down for my grandmother. But then something else amazing happens that stops me to a crawl. A rusty bike speeds past me down the side-walk ridden by the kid with the wild head of hair.

He's weaving in and out of the other people on the sidewalk like he's done this a hundred times before. He catches up to the small boy with my bag, wheels around in front of him and stops him dead in his tracks. The boy starts to back up, but the older boy grabs him by the shirt and motions to him to hand over the bag.

I start walking toward them and get close enough to see the older boy slap the younger one on the back of his head, give him a crumbled up lira bill (I know it's money by the happy look on the kids face), and send him on his way by giving him a playful kick on his backside. The older boy sees me coming and quickly turns away from me as he puts a hand in his pants pocket.

Oh great, he didn't take that away from the little boy to give to me, he took it so he could have it for himself. I stop walking, just waiting for him to jump on his bike and take off again.

But the boy turns back to me and smiles, motioning me to come forward. He then puts the bag over his head, picks up his bike, and starts walking in my direction.

I meet him halfway and he takes my bag from around his neck and gives it to me with a slight bow. "For you."

"Thank you," is all I can think to say. I stare at him a minute and rummage in my bag for my notebook. *Ingilizce biliyor musunuz?* I say, reading from my notebook.

He smiles. "My English very good," he says. "Sorry for boy. He should not work..." He hesitates, then he sees my grandma Agee as she steps up next to us, a bit out of breath.

"You got it back?" she asks.

I turn so she can see it hanging around me again.

"Thank you, young man," she says to the boy. "Can I pay ya something for your trouble?" She starts to dig in her purse for her wallet.

"No need. No need." He looks at me and I swear his cheeks pink up. "My pleasure."

The boy gets back on his bike and looks at us again. "Enjoy Istanbul," he says, then he rides off.

I run after him. "What's your name?" I yell.

He circles around a couple of people on the sidewalk and rides back to stop right next to me. He is three or four inches taller than me and he has a pleasant expression on his face. For some reason I can hear my heart pounding in my ears and I feel really hot, like the sun is beaming down just on me.

"Yusuf," is all he says. Then he smiles and rides

away, waving his hand in the air without turning around.

"I would guess you're still hungry," Grandma Agee says, stepping up to me again.

"I'm famished," I say, forgetting all about the question I was going to ask her. Getting my bag stolen, meeting the boy on the bike, and getting my bag back all in a matter of minutes has my mind reeling and my stomach growling.

After I wolf down a new sandwich, we spend the rest of the day walking the grounds and halls of yet another amazing sight: the Topkapi Palace. It's a huge place, over 400,000 square meters, which is like four football fields square. A lot of the palace is made up of gardens, but there is another mosque inside the palace walls, along with a hospital, a treasury (where the Sutlan kept his valuables), a mint (where he had his gold coins made), a building where the sultan and his family lived (called a harem), and a building just for cooking, just to name a few. It's like a city within a city.

A

That night we plan to eat dinner at our hotel again because we are just too tired to do anything else. While we're in our room getting ready for dinner, our phone rings. Grandma and I look at each other like a fire alarm has gone off and we don't know what valuables we want to grab first. Grandma walks over to the phone and picks it up.

"Yes, this is she."

Grandma Agee looks at me and makes an *I don't know who this is* face.

Then she straightens as the voice on the other end says something else to her. "Yes. Yes, I'll take it."

Grandma holds her hand over the receiver and turns to me. "I'll be a little bit, Agnes. Why don't ya go down and get us a table."

Me? A twelve-year-old? Get a table? Now that's odder than an eight-dollar bill, as my father used to say. "Sure. Let me just get my bag." I walk over to my bed to grab my bag when I spy a drinking glass on the nightstand and get a brilliant idea. I put the bag over my head and shoulder and walk out the door, with Grandma Agee watching my every move.

I close the door behind me but I don't go downstairs, I run down the hall looking for an open room. I'm lucky enough to find one three doors down. I knock quietly and when there is no answer, I peek inside. *Yes!* There on the dresser, is another glass. I snatch it up and run out of the room, hoping I won't run into the room's owner on the way out.

I make it back to our door without seeing anyone and quietly place the open end of the glass on the door and place my ear on the bottom end of the glass. I instantly hear Grandma's muffled voice.

"I'll have to think of something for my grandchild to do while I'm gone. I don't want to leave her sitting in the hotel room all day."

There is a silence, then she speaks again. "That's a good idea. I'll ask Vasil, the hotel manager, to set that up for me. Where and when shall we meet?"

There is another pause and I assume she's getting her instructions. "Will Vasil know where the consulate is?"

The consulate!

"Wonderful. I really appreciate your help in this matter. My daughter-in-law isn't even aware of this, but my son's death was...let's just say very suspicious."

It's at this point that the glass drops to the floor with a thud. I stare at the door, knowing Grandma must have heard the thud, even if it fell on the carpeted hallway. I don't have time to think about what I just heard. I pick up the glass and race down the hall. The room I took the glass from is now closed, so I set it on the floor just to the side of the door and run for the stairway, hoping against hope that I can get out of there before Grandma Agee opens the door to our room, looking for the source of the noise.

I make it to the stairwell and practically fly down the five flights of steps as fast as my legs will take me. I don't wait to catch my breath until I'm in front of the pretty restaurant hostess. I have to lean on my legs a minute before I can speak.

"Are you all right?" she asks.

I put up my hand in the universal sign of *just give me a minute*. It's kind of like the universal choking sign we learned in first aid at school. Everyone knows when you put your hands up to your throat and bug your eyes out, you're choking, no matter what language you speak.

"Sorry," I say, still panting. "My grandma will be down in a few minutes, but she wanted me to get a table for us."

"Your parents won't be eating with you?" she asks.

I stare at this woman dumbfounded. Just my luck, she remembered that I was looking for my parents yesterday. I'll have to put this parent thing to rest right now or the rest of our stay here I'll have to be thinking up excuses for why my mom and dad aren't with me.

"My parents had to go home...because my brother has...typhus," I finally get out. "But they didn't want me to catch it so they left me here with my grandmother."

I had to think up something that sounded bad enough for them to leave but not take me with so typhus came to mind. I don't really know what typhus is, I never took the time to look it up, and I am hoping she doesn't either. I had read it in a book about WWI once and it just popped into my head.

"Oh, I'm so sorry," she says, concern filling her face.

Yes! I think. *It worked. Parents gone for the duration!* [*n: the length of time that something exists or lasts*]

"Right this way," she says and immediately leads me to a table as if she wants to get away from me as quick as she can, in case it's catching somehow.

Five minutes later, Grandma Agee appears.

"Sorry to keep ya waitin', dear," she says as she sits down. "It was rather an important phone call and I had ta talk with Vasil."

Oh yeah, the phone call! How had I forgotten about the phone call? "I hope it wasn't bad news or...or something," I say, fishing for a way to get Grandma to say something about my dad's "very suspicious" death.

"No, no. Nothing like that." She puts her napkin in her lap. Then Grandma looks at me and tips her head, as if she's thinking. "Actually...it was a rug dealer I had been told about. It's one of the reasons I came here. Did ya know Turkey is famous for its wool rugs?"

"No, I didn't," is what I say. *Yeah, you came to see a rug dealer and I'm a monkey's uncle*, is what I am thinking.

"I'm scheduled ta meet with him tomorrow and it's quite a ways outside the city, so it's gonna take all day."

"That's all right. I won't mind seeing a bit of the countryside," I say. *I'm not letting you out of my sight after what you said about Dad!*

"Oh, you won't have to come with, Agnes. I wouldn't put you through that. Vasil has set up a boat trip for you on the Bosporus. He said it is one of the best ways to see the city." Then Grandma picks up the menu and looks through it as if twelve-year-olds frequently take solo boat trips in foreign countries.

We'll see about that.

А

The next morning, while Grandma Agee is still

asleep, I put my plan in place. I had already taken the thermometer out of the medicine cabinet when I got up to use the bathroom just a minute ago, along with a washcloth I soaked in the hottest water I could stand.

Grandma wakes up and I roll away from her and moan.

"Are ya all right, Agnes?"

I moan again, put the hot cloth to my head, drop it to the floor, put the prewarmed thermometer in my mouth, and roll on my back. "I don't think so," I mumble through the thermometer. I take it out and look at it. "I've got a fever."

Grandma is standing next to me now and I hand her the glass tube.

"My, ya do have a fever." She sits down on my bed and feels my forehead. "And you're warm and clammy, too." She sighs and I can tell she's trying to think about what to do about her important meeting today.

"But you don't have to postpone your meeting... with the rug man," I say in a weak voice. "I'll just stay in my room and sleep. If I need anything, I can call room service."

She holds my hand and stares at me. Luckily it's the one that held the washcloth, so that's clammy and warm too. It takes her a few minutes to speak, so I close my eyes and pretend I drift off.

"I suppose you're right. It's best if ya just sleep."

My heart does a somersault and it takes a lot of effort not to smile. I open my eyes half way and nod as if I'm too tired to wake up all the way.

"But we'll start with an aspirin and a glass'a water," she says as she stands and heads for the bathroom, only to be back a few second later with a bottle and a glass of water.

I swallow it down, since I know acetylsalicylic acid (aka – also known as – aspirin) won't hurt me even if I'm not sick. It's one of the most versatile drugs known to man with probably the least side effects, if you don't take a ton of it, of course. How do I know this, you ask? Well, it's not the first time someone gave me aspirin. I had a fever last year, a real one that time, and my mom gave me aspirin. When I was feeling good enough to read again but not good enough to go back to school, I looked it up in the encyclopedia. It's based on a chemical found in the bark of a willow tree and it's been used in one form or another for thousands of years. In fact, the Romans even took some form of acetylsalicylic acid. So it's fitting that here, in the one-time capital of the Roman Empire, that they have a supply of it in their medicine cabinets. There I go, making another connection from way back then to present day. This place is so cool!

"How long do you think you'll be gone?" I ask.

"I don't think I'll be back until late afternoon, so if ya wake up and feel like eatin', just call down for some soup and crackers. Just have them leave it outside your door. No sense in lettin' them know you're alone. I'm sure it would be fine, but I think your mother would prefer it. Don't you?"

I nod my head vigorously, then remember I'm supposed to be sick, so I put my hand on my fore-head and moan again.

A

I have to pretend to sleep while Granny gets dressed. I can see her through slit eyes, looking at me just before she leaves, like she's contemplating waking me up but decides against it.

I wait a good ten minutes before I even try to sit up, then I dress in the bathroom, just in case she has forgotten something and comes back to the room. Even sick girls have to pee.

I'm up, dressed, and I've downed the two rolls I

managed to slip into my blouse at dinner the night before and I'm ready to go.

Now to find out where the consulate is. I'm sitting on Grandma's bed, staring out the sliding glass door to our balcony thinking when I spy the notepad and pen next to the phone. Didn't Hercule Poirot, the detective in one of Agatha Christie's mystery stories, find a clue by looking at a blank notepad? I pick it up and sure enough, if I angle it just right, I can see the indents of Grandma's writing on the pad. I pull a pencil out of my bag and skim over the writing very lightly with the edge of the pencil lead.

Mr. Allen Brooks
US Consulate General
Istinye 34460

I write down the name and address in my own notepad and quietly leave the room. I cross the lobby only when I can see Vasil busy with a customer. Baris, the bellboy, sees me, but I figure he's safe, so I smile and wave. He smiles and waves back.

I step out of the hotel and breathe a sigh of relief: One obstacle taken care of. I decide I will use some of the money Mother gave me for a taxi. I don't know where Istinye Street is, of course, and I didn't write down the translation for "Take me to..." in my composition notebook from the travel guide before I left Wisconsin. Never in my wildest dreams would I have thought I'd be traveling alone. But then I would never have guessed that my father had died under suspicious circumstances, either. Desperate times called for desperate measures. I had heard or read that somewhere and if it fit anywhere, it fit here. I'm desperate to know what happened to my dad, so I'm going to do everything I can to follow Grandma Agee.

I look right, step off the hotel stoop, then remember to check my bag for my room key. I need to be back before Grandma, and I want to make sure I can get back into the room. I see the key, so I look left and head for the curb so I can hail a taxi like Vasil did for us yesterday, but I don't quite make it there.

Next thing I know, I'm on the ground with Yusuf and his bike on top of me. Yusuf lifts himself up on his hands just enough to look me in the face. Neither of us speaks for a good ten minutes. Okay, it's probably more like one minute, but it feels like ten.

"You again?" I say.

Yusuf pushes his bike off his back, then stands and reaches out his hand to help me up.

"Beg your pardon, miss. You saw me, yes, but you walked to my bike."

I stand and brush off my skirt. He didn't say that quite correctly but I get what he meant. "I guess I did see a bike a ways off but I got distracted. I do that a lot," I say and look down at my saddle shoes, embarrassed.

"Are you good?" he asks, then hesitates. "I do not know what you call yourself."

"I'm Agnes, Agnes Kelly," I say, holding out my hand for him to shake. "And I'm fine."

"Please to meet you, Agnes Kelly." When he says my first name, it comes out like "Agniece" because of his accent but I kind of like it, so I don't correct him. He looks behind me. "Where is your mother?"

"My grandmother, actually. She's...she's on her way to the US Consulate." I pause a moment and realize the answer to my question may have just run right into me. I dig out my notepad and show Yusuf the address. "Do you know where this is?"

It takes him a minute, then shakes his head. "This is not in the city, I do not think."

My shoulders droop and I almost drop my notepad. "Darn. I need to follow my grandmother, but she can't know I'm following her." I hesitate but then decide to go on. "You see, my father died recently and my grandmother th18treet, around the corner, and out of sight.

"Well, I guess he *doesn't* understand English," I say out loud. *I guess I'm on my own again. Carpe diem, Seize the day!* I think to myself. *I'll just flag down a taxi like I had planned on earlier and hope I have enough money for the trip.*

I step up to the curb and wave my hand at a passing yellow taxi but it doesn't seem to notice me at all. A minute later a second one drives by but the driver doesn't even look my way. I see another one coming up so I put one foot out in the street and wave both arms this time and the driver slows, but once he gets a good look at me, he speeds up and drives right on by. *Foiled again!* The Turkish boy just left me, I'm too young to hail a taxi on my own, and the clock is ticking. How am I going to get to the consulate and find out who Allen Brooks is and get back here before Grandma does? If Grandma Agee finds out something important about my father's death, she's not going to tell me about it. She didn't tell my mother, her own daughter-in-law, about why she was coming to Turkey, why would she tell me anything.

Remember those tears I told you that would come out of nowhere? Well, they are now filling my eyes, ready to fall out onto my cheeks. I'm all alone in a strange country and I don't know where else to turn.

I pull a handkerchief out of my purse to blow my nose, but there is something that's bunching the handkerchief together. I know it's not a dried booger because it's a clean hanky. I try to see what's holding it in a wad and I find a fuzzy, orange Lifesaver candy I was saving for later. Well, it's later and now it's no good. Just like my plan, no good at all. I stand up and shake the handkerchief hard, upset with my plan, upset with my Lifesaver, upset with my father for dying so early. The tears are coming harder now and I don't notice the taxi that has pulled up right next to me until it honks its horn.

Did I just wave down a taxi with my handkerchief? But when I step closer and look inside, I realize I didn't. Yusuf is sitting right next to the taxi driver and he has a big grin on his face.

"What you waiting for?" he says and motions me into the cab.

I get in the back seat, and we're off to the races.

Yusuf turns around in his seat as I blow my nose on the part of my handkerchief that isn't orange and sticky. "This is happy for you, yes?" he asks, obviously pleased with himself.

I smile at him. "Yes, I am very happy. Thank you, Yusuf," I say and softly touch his arm.

"Agniece Kelly, this is Kareef," he says, looking at the driver. "He is my friend."

"Hello," is all Kareef says. He has an off-white colored turban on his head and he looks different than Yusuf or Vasil, so I think he is a foreigner too.

"*Merhaba*," I say, and Yusuf beams at my attempt at the use of his language.

Kareef just nods and smiles, in what I've come to understand is universal for "I don't want to be rude and say I don't understand you, but I don't understand you." I did the same thing just yesterday when I was asking for directions to the bathroom.

We weave our way through town faster than the day before as Yusuf points out various sights he thinks would interest me. As we pass over the mouth of the Golden Horn, Yusuf tells me this is the Galata Bridge. It's a very old and famous bridge that is very wide to accommodate [*v: to provide room for*] cars, trucks, a cable car, and a wide sidewalk, which at this moment is full of people. Not far off the bridge we turn right, taking a road that runs right alongside the Bosporus. Sitting between the road and the water's edge we pass a boxy and ornate looking building.

This is Dolmabahce Palace," Yusuf explains.

"Was home of six different sultans!" A bit farther up the road we see the Ciragan Palace – also built by a sultan – that Yusuf says is now an expensive hotel. Not too far from the hotel is the Bosporus Bridge, which looks kind of like the Golden Gate Bridge but it's not red. We drive another twenty minutes north and we come upon something that looks like part of a medieval fortress with stone towers and walls that Yusuf calls the Fortress of Europe. The other side of the Bosporus – the other part of Istanbul – is close enough at this point that I can see a similar structure on the opposite bank. I wonder if they had some kind of toll bridge or a robe ferry to charge people to take their horse and cart across the water when the sultans built these stone fortresses long ago.

I look at my Mickey Mouse watch and I notice that it's almost ten. I imagine Grandma took this same route, but I doubt she allowed the driver to travel at the same rate of speed, so hopefully we are making up for some lost time. I don't know how I am going to get into the consulate, but I'm not going to worry about that now. I'll think of something.

Before I know it we're pulling into the parking lot of a very modern looking building that sits in a small, protected bay. Yusuf says something to Kareef and we drive to the back of the parking lot. Yusuf turns to me again.

"We are here."

I swallow hard and open the door to get out. Yusuf gets out as well, leans in his window and talks to the driver a minute before he turns to me.

"You're coming with me?" I ask.

He straightens up and grins. "Of course. I am interpreter!" He tucks in the tails of his blue shirt. It is not a new looking shirt, but it's clean, as are his pants. I just hope they don't look down as far as his shoes. I think he's about worn those out.

"That would be wonderful, Yusuf," I say, and I feel like a big weight has been lifted off my shoulders.

"Kareef will wait for us here."

"So what should we do?"

"Follow me," he says without hesitation and he heads to the back of the building. We follow a service drive up to a row of five large garbage cans and see smoke wafting from behind them. Yusuf motions me to hug a row of dense bushes along the drive and we walk slowly toward the smoke until we spot a group of nicely dressed people wearing nametags, sitting on a bench smoking cigarettes. We wait five minutes and they stamp out their cigarette butts and walk back into the building. Yusuf opens the lids to two garbage cans. When he doesn't like what he sees, he goes to a third and smiles. He pulls out two handfuls of mostly wilted blooms and within a few minutes he has put together a lovely bouquet.

We enter the building through the same door the employees went through and end up in a long, empty hallway.

"Leave to me," Yusuf says, then gives me a wink.

It takes us a while, but we eventually end up in the main waiting room. I grab Yusuf's arm and stop him from entering the lobby. My grandmother is sitting there waiting. Eventually a woman steps up to her and they head down the opposite hallway and turn the corner. When we walk into the lobby, I notice a directory hanging in a glass case on a wall by the entrance. I grab Yusuf's arm and lead him over to the directory. I find the name I wrote down from our hotel notepad and find the associated room number. Unfortunately it doesn't say what Mr. Brooks does at the consulate. I take a deep breath and we walk up to the main desk.

"Excuse me, we have a flower delivery for Mr. Allen Brooks."

The woman at the desk looks at Yusuf, who smiles broadly and holds out his bouquet.

It takes her a minute but she finally answers.

"He is in room 126. Down the hall and fourth door on your left," she says and goes back to the work on her desk.

Office number 126 has a door right next to 125. Both doors are open. Yusuf motions for me to wait while he walks past both doors and walks back to me.

"Your grandmother is not in room, just office woman," he says with a questioning look on his face.

I lean against the wall and sigh, wondering what to do next. I haven't come this far just to lose her and my chance to find out what happened to my father. I'm about to suggest we go back to the lobby and ask the receptionist where my grandmother might be when I hear her voice. I plaster myself against the wall and Yusuf does the same.

"I am sorry too, Mr. Brooks, but the fact remains that we were told he was workin' in Turkey when he had his car accident, but the letter I received from him the day he died was from Norway. There is something fishy about this and it smells to high heaven."

The government lied to us?! Our government doesn't lie to people. Why would they do that? I try and keep up with current events and I could understand the Russian government lying. They probably even lied about that cosmonaut orbiting the earth. I know the

Russians sent a dog into space but I don't think they'd send a man.

"My hands are tied, Mrs. Kelly," a deep voice says.

"One way or another, I plan on gettin' to the bottom of this," Grandma Agee says.

"I'm sorry you came all this way," the man says.

In the silence that follows, Yusuf pulls me into the adjacent [*adj: close or near*] office. He puts me in a chair just inside the door then walks up to the secretary's desk and addresses her by name. I wonder how he knows this woman's name until I see she has a nameplate on her desk.

I am not sure what his plan is and I'm distracted by my grandmother's voice again, so I don't listen to him to find out. I lean closer so I can hear Grandma Agee better.

"Miss Lang, I wonder if ya could do an old lady a favor. My son Patrick had a partner in Turkey who sent me a nice card after my son's passing, but I have seemed ta have misplaced it. Would ya happen to have his address and phone number? Since I came all this way, I'd like to take the opportunity ta stop by and say thank you in person."

There is a brief silence before the woman responds. "I...I guess that would be fine."

There is another pause, probably while she is

writing down the man's information, then my grandmother says thank you.

"Can ya spell his name out for me?" Grandma says. "Since I don't have the card with me, I don't remember how his name is spelled.

"Thank you. You've been so helpful. You have a nice day, now."

I take that as my cue to move a couple seats farther from the doorway. Yusuf turns toward me and I see the secretary look in the cupboard behind her for an empty vase to put her new flowers in. I give him a thumbs up and we both move toward the door. Yusuf holds me back while he peers down the hallway. He nods his head for the all clear sign, and I wave at the secretary who just now has noticed there was someone else in her office. I leave before she has a chance to ask me any questions.

We turn in the opposite direction of the lobby and my grandmother. We find a duplicate back door to the one we entered and head back to our waiting taxi.

We both get in the back seat this time and Yusuf tells the driver something in Turkish and we turn and speed out of the lot. I look back at the entrance to see a taxi pull up in front of my grandmother.

"You found out about your father?" Yusuf asks.

"Not quite yet, but from the way my grandmother was talking to that secretary, I'm guessing she isn't done asking questions."

"Should Kareef follow grandmother?"

I look at my watch and shake my head. "She wants to meet up with my father's partner in Turkey but it's too late for her to be meeting him today. She said she was going to be back to our hotel by late afternoon, so we better just go back to the Zanzibar." I leave out the part about her wanting to get back and check on her sick granddaughter.

Yusuf notices my watch. My parents bought it for me when I turned ten but they got it a bit big so I could grow into it. "Mickey Mouse! I like Mickey Mouse and Donald Duck. I see cartoons before movies. John Wayne is good," he says, making gun sounds and shooting bad guys with his hands. "And Humphrey Bogart." Yusuf has a little trouble pronouncing Bogart's first name. "Here's looking at you, kid," he says and gives me a wink.

Yusuf is quoting Humphrey Bogart from the movie Casablanca that Peggy and I was a few weeks ago. I have to laugh at his imitation of Mr. Bogart. I've never heard it with a Turkish accent.

"You see American movies?" I say, surprised. I

wouldn't have thought they would play American movies in Turkey.

"That's where I learn English so good," he says with a smile. "Movies and tourists."

I nod and smile back. I have to wonder what a boy who steals breadbaskets and knows how to get himself into the back door of a government building does for the tourists. It doesn't really matter to me, though. I don't know what I would have done without him. Now I only have to figure out how I can get Grandma Agee to take me to meet my father's Turkish partner. He's sure to know something about what happened to him.

We pull up to the hotel in record time. I rummage in my bag and pull out my lira bills.

"No, no!" Yusuf says, pushing my hand away. "You are guest."

I look down at his shoes. The shoestrings have at least two knots in them on each foot.

"How about half the fare?" I say, handing fifty lira out to him. He looks at Kareef, who is looking encouragingly at Yusuf to accept the money.

"Okay. This is good for Kareef," he says, then takes a few crumpled liras out of his own pocket and gives it all to the driver.

We both get out of the cab and walk into the hotel.

"Do you need help tomorrow?" Yusuf asks.

"I might," I say. "But how can I contact you to let you know?"

"Hold your horses," he says again. He looks around the room and finally sees what he's looking for. He walks over to the bellboy and puts his arm around his shoulder like they are old chums. He uses his hands a lot to gesture right, then left twice and up, followed by three fingers and a smile. When the boy smiles back, Yusuf claps him on the back and walks back over to me. "I tell Baris. He knows how to get me."

I look at my watch again, then at the entrance doors. "I really need to get going, Yusuf. Thank you so much for all your help."

"Of course!" he says and I can tell by his expression that he means it. "Here's looking at you, kid," he says in his best Bogart accent, then gives me a two-finger salute and runs out of the lobby.

Once I'm back in my room, I put on my pajamas and hop in bed. I decide against pretending to still be asleep, so I get out of bed, get my *Arabian Nights* books, and turn to *Aladdin and his Magic Lamp*. I want to find out if there are really any flying carpets in this story. Ends up I am kind of tired from my rather exciting day and not sleeping well last night, so Grandma Agee has to wake me up, my book open in my lap.

Grandma sits down hard on her bed. She looks more tired than me. "How ya feelin', Agnes?"

"Better, actually. Did you get the rug you wanted?"

"The rug! Oh, yes, the rug. No, I didn't get the rug I wanted." She stares at me a minute. "Do ya mind awfully, sweetheart, if I try again tomorrow. Vasil told me about a different rug shop, but this one is in town, so I'll only be gone for two...three hours."

"Sure, Grandma, I don't mind. I didn't get very far in my book, anyway." Which, of course, was quite true.

"How about we have dinner brought up ta the room. I don't feel up to goin' out this evenin' and I doubt you do either."

"Sure, that'd be fine."

We end up having our own little Turkish dinner on our small balcony. She orders something called *meze* (mez-a) off the room service menu after the kitchen recommended it. When the food arrives, Grandma brings out two bed pillows for us to sit on. She puts a platter covered with small bowls of various spreads and cooked vegetables between us and plates with flat bread in our laps as we talk about what we saw in the mosques and the Topkapi Palace the day before. Even though I still don't know any more about my dad or what happened to him, with the sights and sounds of the large city lit up as our exotic background, I still consider myself pretty lucky.

Chapter 6

Grandma is up early, so I dress quickly and join her for breakfast in the hotel restaurant. I have to think of a way to find out where she is going. We start our meal and I take my first stab at it.

I look up and out the large windows that line the front of the restaurant. "Looks like a nice day. Maybe you can walk to the rug shop and see a few things along the way that we can check out when you get back," I say and take a bite of my toast.

"No. No. It's too far ta walk," she says, putting down her coffee cup. "I'll just give Vasil the address and he can call me a taxi."

Vasil! I can get the address from Vasil! Problem solved.

We finish eating and Grandma puts her napkin on the table "So I'll just meet ya back here in two, maybe three hours then; say eleven-thirty at the latest."

"Sure. Maybe I'll get my book and read in the lobby. That way I can watch the people coming and going if I get bored with my reading."

"Good idea," she says and stands.

In the lobby she kisses my head and walks over to Vasil, who never seems to take a day off. I wave to her as she leaves, then I walk over to the bellboy.

"Excuse me, Baris, but my friend from yesterday, Yusuf?" I don't know if the boy understands me but he seems to perk up at the mention of Yusuf's name. "Can you call him for me?" I extend my pinky finger and thumb to make a phone out of my hand and put it to my ear.

"Of course. Of course," he says enthusiastically. But he doesn't go over to the phone on the lobby desk, he walks into the restaurant.

"Oh jeez, not this again." I sit down in the nearest chair to wait and see if he actually understood me or if he comes back with something off the menu.

But what he walks out with is neither Yusuf nor some sort of Turkish delight. He is pulling a young boy by the hand, a boy that is in a worn outfit similar to Yusuf's but he looks of no relation to him. The bellboy goes through the same hand gestures Yusuf did the day before and holds up three fingers at the end of his explanation. He pulls out a coin and stuffs it in the kid's hand, and the boy immediately runs out the front doors.

The bellboy turns to me and bows, then is pulled away with the yell of "Baris" from Vasil behind the front desk.

I run up the steps to my room, stuff my book in my bag, and run back downstairs.

I walk quickly up to Vasil and put on my best worried face. I have my wallet in my hand.

"Vasil, I wonder if you can help me. My grandmother has left without her wallet. Can you please give me the address of where she's going so I can take it to her?"

"Oh, this is not good," he says, putting a hand to his cheek. "She was going to the Spice Market so she is sure to need her wallet. Maybe if you go quickly, you can catch her," he says as he starts to walk around the front desk. Just then, a young couple walks in the front doors with suitcases in hand.

"Oh dear, I must take care of this lovely couple," Vasil whispers to me. He turns and yells behind us, "Baris!" And he does his usual come here hand gesture but this time more rapidly. "Come, come, come," he says, urging Baris forward. "Please take the Miss and get her a taxi to the Spice Market. Ask the driver to stay and wait for her. If the Miss does not find her grandmother, she will be immediately returning to the hotel." He then looks at me and nods.

I know Vasil would normally give these instructions in Turkish, so I assume he is saying this in English partly for my benefit.

I smile politely. "*Teşekkürler*, Vasil," I say as best I can. (I had Vasil teach me how to say thank you in Turkish – *tay-sheck-cue-lar.*) "Grandmother will appreciate it."

Vasil bows and I walk outside with Baris. We are greeted by Yusuf's smiling face. Today he's wearing a t-shirt with Elvis Presley on the front. He bows deeply and sweeps a hand down and out as if he is an Old English gentleman.

"And how may I help Miss Agniece?"

I put my hand over my mouth to stifle [v: *to not allow yourself to do or express something*] a laugh.

"My grandmother is meeting someone in the Spice Market. Can you take me there?"

"Of course" he says, "But you not want her to see."

"Right!" I say. *This kid doesn't miss a thing!*

"So we must hold our horses first."

I cock my head, unsure about what he is trying to say. "I guess," is all I can come up with.

Yusuf takes that as a correct answer and proceeds to pull his bike from its resting place against the building. He lets me know that I'm to sit on the seat.

At this moment I am glad I decided to wear my jeans instead of a skirt. I didn't know what I would be getting into today so I wanted to be able to move without worrying about my skirt flying up in my face. Dresses and skirts are nice when it's hot out, but most of the rest of the time, they aren't very handy.

Yusuf straddles the bike, holds it while I sit on the seat, then we're off, moving down the street at Yusuf's usual rapid pace. He has to stand the whole time, of course, so I hold onto his belt to keep myself from falling off, though I'm able to use my legs a bit as a counter weight.

We weave our way out of the heart of the city to streets that are more and more occupied by people and less and less by cars or trucks. The streets also start to get narrower. The buildings in this part of town are mostly two stories, the second floor built so it hangs out over the first floor, as if they started to build it and decided they wanted more space so they just made the second story wider.

We stop outside of one such building and Yusuf hops off and holds the bike for me to do the same. The wood siding on the building is gray, as if it's very old. It's like many of the others on this narrow street; it is in great need of a good coat of paint.

Yusuf opens the door and waits for me to step inside.

"Where are we?" I ask.

"This my home," he says.

My eyes go wide and I'm stuck in place. What if Yusuf is one of those bad people my mother warned me about? What if it's not his home but some bad-guy hideout?

As I stagnate [*v: to stop developing, progressing, moving etc.*], pondering my next move, four small children plus two that look to be just a bit younger than Yusuf, poke their heads out of the door. They all stare at me as I stare back at them. I eventually manage a smile and a wave at the six young, so-called, hoodlums [*n: tough and violent criminals*]. One of the older boys steps out and starts talking to Yusuf in Turkish as he eyes me suspiciously. Yusuf responds back and ushers them all back through the door, then waits again for me to enter.

The home is small and sparsely furnished, but there isn't a speck of dirt to be seen. The small children, one boy and three girls, gather around Yusuf like he's the pied piper as he digs in his pants pocket and magically pulls out some candy, then two rolls out of his shirt.

I didn't notice those.

He walks up to one of the older boys and drops a wad of crumpled lira into his hands from out of his other pocket. The boy proceeds to pull a jar off a shelf and place the lira inside it.

I know what Yusuf looks like and I know that he isn't what Father Michael would call a saint. What I also now know is that it's not just books people are talking about when they say, you can't judge a book by its cover. I don't know how Yusuf gets his money or his food but now it doesn't seem to matter.

Yusuf then talks to the whole group, who are looking at me as if I'm going to turn into the green monster from the black lagoon at any minute. He eventually says my name and their faces start to melt into small smiles. He talks to the oldest girl, Esma, who is probably only seven, and she smiles broadly at me and runs up a narrow, steep stairway only to be back down a few minutes later with some color-ful clothes in her hands. She thrust them out to me, proud as punch at what she's found.

"*Teşekkürler,* Esma," I say, and she covers her mouth and giggles.

Yusuf walks up to me to inspect the goods. "Is this good?" he says, holding up a scarf and a colorful tunic.

"Good for what?" I ask, still not sure what he has planned.

"For disguise! We go to Spice Market, yes? You must look like Turkish shopper."

"Are these your mother's?"

"No, sister."

"Are you sure she won't mind."

He looks at me puzzled. "She has good mind," he says pointing to his own head.

I try again. "Is she okay for me to wear?" I say in butchered English, as if that is going to help him understand, but amazingly enough, it does.

"Sure, sure. She okay." And he proceeds to take the scarf and tries to put it around my head in the traditional Islamic manner. I've seen many ladies in scarves as we walked the streets on our tours and he isn't even close. The girls are all giggling at his attempt and eventually they shove him aside and all three of them gather around me. I kneel down so they can reach me better and in no time I've got the light- green scarf snug and secure on my head.

I slip the tunic over my head and it hangs down past my knees. I don't think it's supposed to go that far down because Esma runs back upstairs and comes down with a long, black cloth that she puts around my middle. It helps pull the tunic up just enough so it doesn't look like an oversized dress. I look in a small mirror by the door and am amazed at my transformation.

Yusuf stands beside me and looks at me in the mirror. "This is good! No?"

"No? Oh, yes, this is very good!"

"Now I disguise too."

Yusuf bounds up the steps two at a time and comes back wearing a white linen shirt with large, puffy sleeves and a maroon embroidered vest.

"I wear for festivals and holy days," he explains.

He would look quite handsome if his hair wasn't so wild.

"Hold your horses," I say as kind of a joke, using the idiom Yusuf likes to use. I walk over to Esma and whisper to her, doing my best pantomime and she smiles wide in understanding.

She goes back upstairs and returns with a comb and a small, wide-mouthed jar. I open the jar and take a dab of the goop on my fingers. I put it on both of my hands, walk back over to Yusuf, and drag my fingers through his hair. It's not easy, let me tell you. The kid's got more snarls than Medusa. (If you don't know, Medusa is a Greek mythical creature with snakes on her head instead of hair – Cool, huh?!) He puts up with it with nary a grunt, and after I've combed it out, not even his own mother would recognize him, let alone my grandmother.

Yusuf looks at himself in the mirror and is pleased with what he sees. He opens a cupboard in the kitchen and pulls out a mesh bag, takes my bag and puts it inside the mesh bag.

"Now you are Turkish shopper. Let us go!" he says and motions for me to leave the house before him.

As we work our way back to the tourist area of the city, Yusuf turns his head slightly to talk to me.

"Agniece," he says then stops talking, as if he is trying to think of what to say. "When we first meet, in front of mosque, I only see rich American tourist."

I don't consider myself a rich American, but compared to the way Yusuf and his family live, I guess I am. When he bumped into me, I thought he probably lived on the street.

"I bump you and take..."

He hesitates so I interrupt him. I remember him turning away from me after he grabbed my bag from the small boy who took it and how he put his hand in his pocket.

"That's okay, Yusuf. You gave it back to me. No harm done."

Yusuf smiles, then turns and pedals even faster, as if I have just given him wings.

We pull up to a long, two-story, brick building that must be the Spice Market; it is very busy with local people and tourists coming and going. The entrance has three softly pointed arches on its face but only the center arch leads to a long corridor with a similarly pointed, vaulted ceiling. The corridor is maybe only fifteen feet wide with brightly lit shops tightly crammed in on each side. The sights and smells are unbelievable and I don't know how in the world we are ever going to find my grandmother in all of this. My saddle shoes have suddenly become as heavy as cement, and I can't seem to move my feet. I am so overwhelmed [v: *to have too many things to deal with*] by it all.

Yusuf has walked ahead of me but comes back and takes my hand, pulling me along like a lost puppy into the throng of people, who are strolling or gazing at the colorful trays of fruits, spices, or trinkets for sale. I don't resist.

We make our way to a more open area that leads

to an even longer corridor of shops and we stop. Yusuf is looking for my grandmother, but I can't seem to stop looking at all the various things for sale: scarves lined up on poles or piled high on tables; spices of every hue and texture; sweets in any shape or with any filling you could want; lines of colorful ceramic dishes or row upon row of hanging lamps; everything arranged in a pleasing display, optimal [*adj: best or most effective*] for a sale.

Yusuf sees that I am of no use, so he plants me in a small metal chair outside a tea shop.

"I look down here," he says, pointing to the long corridor.

My speech has somehow left me as well as my intellect [*n: the ability to think in a logical way*], so I just nod my head and get distracted again by the things and people all around me.

I am woken out of my trance when a cup of tea is placed in front of me.

"For the Miss?" the young man says, "It is chamomile. Light yet flavorful. You try, you try. It is soothing," he says with a wide smile, lifting the cup up for me to take.

I look around and notice where I'm sitting, in front of a tea shop. I hadn't ordered tea, so I'm not sure what to do, unsure if I will offend him if I don't take it.

"Please, it is free to taste," he says as if he can read my mind.

"Oh, sure," I say and put down my net bag.

I bring it slowly to my lips, noticing the small, handless cup is warm to the touch, when the delicate aroma of sweet mint and licorice fills my nose. I've never had tea before but something Mr. M. said before he took a bite of my grandma Barb's sauerkraut comes to my mind: "When in Rome..." My father's family is Irish, that's why my last name is Kelly but my mother's family is German and French. Grandma Barb was known for her sauerkraut and rib dinner. I like the ribs okay, but the sauerkraut is something only the adults seem to appreciate. Mr. M. liked to try almost anything. He explained to me that the saying is actually "When in Rome, do as the Romans do," which means, when you are in a place that is new to you, you should try and behave like those around you, like the people that live there.

I take a sip of the tea and the warm drink seems to do exactly what the man said; I take a deep breath and melt into my chair. As I take another sip, the young man opens a small wooden box that he is holding in his other hand. It has row upon row of different colored little paper packets. He then starts to tell me all about the different types of teas in each of these little packets.

My eyes go wide and I stare at him like a deer standing in the road when you come upon it at night with your car. *He wants me to buy some tea! I'm not sure I want to buy tea and which one would I buy? Will he get upset if I don't buy his tea after he offered me some for free?!*

I am rescued from my predicament by my Turkish knight in shining armor. Yusuf talks to the young man in Turkish and without so much as a blink of his eye, the young man snaps his box closed and moves on to the next person.

"I find grandmother," he says.

I pick up my bag and follow Yusuf down the long corridor. We stop in front of a spice shop. There are ascending rows of baskets with spices mounded into peaks and a yellow tag sticking out of each one telling you what it is and what it cost. I peer cautiously into the store but don't see her anywhere. I look at Yusuf. He points to the next shop, a pottery shop, and nods his head. I slowly walk around the mounds of colorful spices and can see my grandmother holding a full shopping bag and talking with a tall Turkish man. She obviously went shopping before she had her rendez-vous [*n: a meeting with someone that is arranged for a particular time and place and that is often secret*].

I pull my scarf a little tighter to my face and walk closer to the storefront, pretending that I'm looking at the spices next door.

"Thank ya for your help, Nero. I knew there was somethin' not right about my son's death. And I tell you, I am not gonna stop there. I am gonna find out what happened ta him."

I swallow hard and step a bit closer.

"All I can tell you...let me rephrase that. All I know, Mrs. Kelly, is that his last location was in Norway. I can't tell you what his mission was, that is top secret, but if I knew anything about his death, I promise, I would tell you. You know as much as I do on that score."

Mission?! Top secret?! I turn and look at Yusuf, who is standing next to me listening as well. "My dad sold insurance!" I whisper, my eyes bugging out of my head. "Why would he be on a top secret mission?!"

Then I freeze.

Grandma Agee and Nero have walked out of the store and are standing just behind us.

My heart starts to race and I bend over as if I am going to smell the spices in front of me.

"I appreciate ya going out of your way, Nero. I know my son didn't like keepin' his family in the dark, but he did like his job in the CIA."

I inhale quickly from the shock of my grandma's words. My father said he worked for the government helping people sign up for insurance policies. Now I come to find out he worked for the CIA!

Unfortunately, when I inhaled, I took in a nose full of the yellow spice that I was bending over, a spice that was now about to come right back out.

I try to hold it, but I can't help myself. I sneeze right back into that mound of yellow spice.

At that, everyone around me, including my grandmother and Nero, look in my direction. Now I'm done for.

Chapter 7

The jig is up. I've been found out. I have botched [*v: to do something badly because of carelessness or lack of skill*] the job. I had wanted to find out what had happened to my dad and what I find out instead is he worked for the CIA and now my grandmother knows that I know too. Now she will never trust me again, she'll never tell me anything she finds out about what happened to my dad. I turn toward Grandma Agee with downcast eyes, ready to be chastised [*v: to be criticized harshly for doing something wrong*] in front of Nero, in front of Yusuf, in front of everyone!

But what I hear instead is a stifled snicker. I look up and my grandmother has her hand over her mouth, trying not to laugh. She looks at Nero, who has more of a disgusted look on his face, and the pair turn and leave the pottery shop and start walking down the corridor together.

I look over at Yusuf, who is also trying to restrain himself. "Very good disguise, Agniece."

I give him a questioning stare and he turns me toward the glass front of the pottery shop. My grandmother didn't recognize me not because of my brilliant disguise. She didn't recognize me because my face is covered in yellow turmeric.

A

Once we get the turmeric off my face, I notice Mickey's hands are creeping up toward eleven and we rush out of the Market and back to my hotel. I hand Yusuf his sister's scarf and take off my belt and tunic and put it all in the net shopping bag.

I stare at Yusuf, unsure what to say, so I don't say anything; I give him a hug instead. He stands stiffly and smiles when I finally release him.

"Thank you so much, Yusuf. I don't know what it means that my father worked for the CIA, but I'm guessing it had something to do with what happened to him."

I walk back toward the front entrance of the hotel, then stop and turn back.

"I've got one more day here before we have to go back home. It would be great if we just happen to meet you on the street again, you know, by accident or something."

"Ah, yes, by accident," he says with a nod. "But not with the bike," he jokes.

"Yes, not an accident with the bike," I say and rub my backside.

I wave and run into the hotel, pulling my book out of my shoulder bag.

A

Grandma and I have kebabs for lunch, a traditional Turkish dish, Vasil explained to us later. A kebab is basically meat cooked on a stick. When you get it like we did, as we were walking along the footpath next to the Bosporus, you eat it right off the stick. What a great idea! It was so good I order the same thing that night in the hotel restaurant. In the restaurant they bring it to me on a stick on top of some rice, then they pull it off the stick for me so I can eat it in a more "civilized manner" or so Grandma Agee says. I prefer the stick method myself.

᠕

The next morning we decide to eat our breakfast outside. It is a beautiful day and our last full day in Turkey so neither of us wants to miss a thing. Grandma suggests that we will take the same boat trip up the Bosporus that I was supposed to take when I got sick. Then if we have time, we might go shopping at the Grand Bazaar. I can't tell her that I have already seen part of the sights along the river, so I readily agreed. Things would probably look different from the water, anyway.

"Since it will take a few minutes for our food ta get here, I am gonna go ask Vasil ta set up that boat trip for us," Grandma said. So she stands and walks back into the restaurant.

When she's gone, Yusuf and his bike appear around the block. He sees me and waves. I wave back. He sets his bike against the hotel and walks over to our table. Today he has a picture of the three musketeers on his t-shirt. That explains the elaborate bow I got yesterday. His hair is back to its normal wild mop.

"Are you eating alone?" he asks.

"No, my grandmother just stepped inside for a few minutes. Would you like to meet her?"

"Yes, very much," he says, nodding.

Then he looks out into the street and points. "Oh my! Look at that," he says loudly so everyone sitting outside can hear.

We all turn and look at what Yusuf is pointing at. I don't see anything so I immediately turn back around. Out of the corner of my eye I see Yusuf grabing a piece of bread from the next table with his other hand. Unfortunately, my grandmother is standing directly behind him and sees the same thing and she grabs hold of his wrist.

"I'd drop that if I were you," she whispers in his ear.

He does as he is told and turns to face her.

The people sitting at the table eventually look at Grandma and Yusuf but they didn't seem to notice what had just happened; they go right back to eating their meal.

"Now I think we should take a little stroll into the hotel and have a talk with the manager," Grandma says, her voice still low.

I stand to protest. "Grandma, this is Yusuf, the boy who recovered my bag for me outside of the mosque."

It takes Grandma a moment but she finally does recognize him.

"I invited him to join us for breakfast," I say, hoping both Yusuf and my grandmother don't mind.

"I guess he didn't know what table we were eating at," Grandma says with a smirk and sits down in her seat.

I breathe a sigh of relief that he isn't going to be hauled off to the hoosegow [*n: prison or jail*] and nod my head in the direction of one of the two empty seats. Yusuf picks the one closer to me and farther from my grandmother. About this time the waiter brings us our food. "And the young man will be eating with us as well," my grandmother explains.

Yusuf smiles. "*Menemen lütfen,*" he says without looking at a menu. It's basically scrambled eggs with small bits of tomato, green pepper, and onion in it. It's what I've had each morning and it is quite tasty, even with the glob of what Grandma says is garlic yogurt on top. I don't usually eat vegetables for breakfast, but I promised my grandmother I'd try everything at least once, and the stuff has kind of grown on me. And as Mr. M. said, "When in Rome..."

Grandma doesn't speak until the waiter comes back with Yusuf's food.

"So Yusuf, how do ya happen to know where Agnes and I are stayin'?"

Yusuf looks at me with wide eyes, obviously unsure what to say. This time I am his knight or lady knight, if there is such a thing.

I slowly set down my fork. I know I am jeopardizing [*v: to put (something or someone) in danger*] any chances of Grandma Agee ever telling me anything about what happened to my father and that I'm going to be in hot water for what I am about to say, but for all Yusuf has done for me, I can't let him be the one that gets in trouble. It was all my idea.

"He's been helping me, Grandma. He doesn't live too far away, and I saw him riding his bike by the hotel the other day," I say, not giving her all the details. Maybe if I don't have to tell her everything, then Grandma won't be as mad at me. "I asked him to help me follow you to the Spice Market."

She squints at me. "Were you the young girl who had a face full of yellow spice?"

I nod my head.

"Why did ya follow me?"

I look at my grandmother a moment, trying to decide what to say. Should I confess everything? The fact that I listened in on her conversation and overheard her say that my father's death was suspicious; the fact that I followed her to the US Consulate and found out he actually died in Norway and not in

Turkey like they told us; and finally the fact that I found out that my father did not sell insurance but he worked for the CIA. I wonder what else about my father don't I know? I decide to start with answering her question.

"Because I heard you on the phone say Dad's death was suspicious."

Grandma's expression doesn't change.

"Did ya follow me to the consulate too?"

I hesitate. "Yes. Yusuf knows a taxi driver...."

My grandmother puts up her hand to stop me. "Spare me the details, Agnes." She looks over at Yusuf, then at me and shakes her head. I hang my head in shame.

I brace myself, ready for what I know is coming. I pretended I was sick. I took a ride from a stranger. I put on a disguise to follow her. I listened in on a private conversation.... It would be a never ending list. I am in such big trouble. I suspect our last day in Istanbul is over before it has even begun. No boat trip on the Bosporus. No shopping at the Grand Bazaar. We're going home as soon as we can pack our things and get a plane out of Turkey. I look at Yusuf. He swallows hard.

"I have to apologize to ya, Agnes. I should have been straight with ya from the start."

My eyes flip to my grandmother and stick there, just like my open mouth is stuck open.

"You obviously are more mature than your twelve years and deserve ta know what's goin' on."

Grandma puts her napkin on the table. "Patrick... your father is not a government insurance salesman; he works...I mean *worked* for the Central Intelligence Agency."

(Grandma's having trouble with the past tense thing too.)

She stops, expecting me to look shocked, so I give her my best surprised face. I don't have to work too hard. I am pretty amazed I'm not getting an earfull like Uncle Bob had. Now I know what he was going to say at the funeral: Since my dad read spy and detective novels as a kid, it wasn't surprising that he got into the business himself.

I don't interrupt Grandma and tell her I know this fact already because maybe she'll tell me something I don't already know. She has my full attention.

"He sent me a letter postmarked from Norway dated the day he died, so I knew somethin' wasn't right. That's why I came to Turkey. I thought if I spoke to the people he worked with here, I could find out somethin' more about what was going on."

"Is that why you talked to his partner in the pottery shop?" I ask.

"How did ya know it was his partner I was talking to?"

Drat, I should have just kept my mouth shut and listened. "I overheard you talking with Miss Lang in Mr. Brooks' office," I say, a bit sheepishly. [No, I didn't sound like a bleating sheep when I said that; *sheepish* is an adjective that means *to show or feel embarrassment especially because you have done something foolish or wrong.*]

Grandma shakes her head again but the look on her face is more like she is amazed at me rather than disgusted.

"I don't remember that we got a card from a man named Nero," I say.

"That's because ya didn't. I didn't know he was workin' with a partner here. That was the only thing Mr. Brooks let slip. I said his partner had sent us a card because I wanted ta get his name and address." Grandma looked a bit embarrassed. "Yes, I shouldn't have lied, but Mr. Brooks wasn't going ta help me so I thought I would try his partner."

"And he was the one that confirmed Dad was in Norway when he got in his accident and not in Turkey."

"Yes, but what Nero Bahar also told me was they were workin' with a man in Norway by the name of Mr. Nicko Borge. He couldn't tell me what they were workin' on; it's top secret. But what he did tell me was that Mr. Borge works in section EI4 of the Norwegian Intelligence Agency."

Yusuf lets out a long, slow whistle, impressed by what my grandmother just said. Both of us look at him. I think we both forgot he was even there. He must have finished his breakfast while he was listening because his plate is completely clean and the tray that had the bread on it is half-empty.

Grandma Agee puts a hand on top of Yusuf's. "Thank you for takin' such good care of my Agnes, Yusuf. My son would have appreciated it as much as I do."

Yusuf smiles. "One of the five pillars of Muslim life is to help the needy, and Agniece was in need," he says and gives me a wink. "Besides, Agniece Kelly is my friend, and that is what friends do."

I give him a wink back.

I suggest to Grandma that it might be nice, as a thank you, to have Yusuf join us on our boat trip. She readily agrees, so we all enjoy a leisurely motor up and down the Bosporus. We stop half way in the trip in Anadolu Kavagi (*anna-doe-lu ca* (like in cat)-*vaa-*

jI) and have lunch. Anadolu Kavagi is a picturesque little city that clings to the edge of the water near the Black Sea and has a 14th-century castle called Genoese Castle (*jen-o-ease*), protecting it from a hilltop just behind it. We have a meal of Turkish *pide* (*pee-day*), which is like our American pizza but shaped like a boat. I don't recognize the stuff on top except the tomatoes, but it tastes good all the same. After lunch Yusuf and I take the roughly half-mile trek to the castle ruins, which sounds easy but it is uphill all the way. Grandma decides to enjoy a cocktail by the waterside while she waits. Before we get back on the boat, we grab a wonderful, sweet flaky thing called baklava from a bakery in town. We bring it on board with us and wash it down with a cup of rosehips tea while we watch the world go by. We have enough time when we step off the boat to do a little souvenir shopping in the Grand Bazaar.

I am glad Yusuf is with us to help us shop. Apparently it's customary to never accept the first price a shopkeeper offers you. In fact, Yusuf motioned for us to leave a couple different shops before the shopkeeper brought his price down to what Yusuf thought it should be. Grandma calls it "haggling," and she says it is important to not look too interested in what you want to buy. She's pretty good at it, too, when she haggles with a shopkeeper to try and buy a rug she actually did want to get. Seems like a lot of rigmarole [*n: a long and compli-cated procedure.*] to me.

Chapter 8

Yusuf meets us bright and early the next morning before our ride to the airport and to home. I suggest to him that we be pen pals, like my teacher Miss Appleton set up for us in the fifth grade. I was a pen pal with Maria Sanchez for about a year. She lives in Chiapas, Mexico. Eventually one of us stopped writing – I can't remember if it was her or me – so we lost touch. Once Yusuf understands what a pen pal is, he thinks it's a good idea. I imagine it costs more than four cents, like within the US, to send a letter to Turkey, but I'm hoping my mom won't mind. I hope Yusuf and I are friends for a very long time.

Before we leave, he pulls a wrapped package from the bag he has over his shoulder.

"It is for you and Grandmother," he says, handing it to me. "It is baklava. You like it much so Esma and Mamma make some for you. It is better than at Anadolu Kavagi."

"I'm sure it is. Thanks, Yusuf!"

Then Yusuf takes off the pendant that hangs around his neck by a round leather cord and places it over my head.

"This from me. It is the evil eye. Everyone in Turkey have this. It gives happiness and protection to beloved ones."

I touch the flat glass pendant and smile. It's round with consecutive [*adj: following one after the other*] dark blue, white, then light blue circles with a black dot in the center. "I'll wear it all the time."

I take a small box out of my bag and I hand it to Yusuf. "This is from me and Grandma."

Yusuf pulls on the string and opens the box. It's my Mickey Mouse watch. Vasil helped Grandma and me find a jewelry shop that changed my small band for one that was made for a boy.

"This is Agniece's watch," he says, a bit confused.

"Yes and now it's Yusuf's watch," I say with a smile. I noticed that Yusuf seems to like anything American: movie stars, cartoon characters, musicians, and what's more American than Mickey Mouse! It looks better on him, anyway.

His face brightens and he gives me a big hug. "Thank you, Agniece Kelly. This is a happy thing!"

My grandmother steps up to us. "Agnes, we have ta go."

We aren't going to be taking the bus back to the airport because Yusuf had called Kareef to take us. She puts out her hand for Yusuf to shake. "It was nice meeting you, Yusuf. You take care of yourself." She walks back and gets into the taxi.

I turn to Yusuf and I feel lost. How do you say goodbye to someone who you just met a few days ago but who feels like a close friend? I would've never guessed that I would be friends with someone like Yusuf, but here we are exchanging gifts and addresses so we can be pen pals.

"You take care of yourself, Yusuf. Thank Esma and your mother for us," I say, holding up the wrapped baklava.

"Here's looking at you, kid," Yusuf says and gives me a two-finger salute.

I smile and salute back. Yusuf gets on his bike and rides off, waving at me without looking back.

I get into the taxi and sigh.

Grandma sets a hand on my leg and gently gives it a squeeze.

It's been the most amazing trip, but strangely enough I am kind of missing my family. My mother mostly, but my brothers, too. When I watched Yusuf interacting with his brothers and sisters, it made me think about my family. I actually missed being able to share some of what I was seeing with my siblings and, of course, Peggy. She's not going to believe what happened with Yusuf and me.

"Agnes, I've been thinkin'. Since the government decided it wasn't important enough ta tell us the truth about where your father died, I am wonderin' what else they might not have told us."

My thoughts exactly! I think as I nod my head in agreement.

"I would like ta find this Mr. Nicko Borge and see what else he knows about Patrick's death." Grandma stops and stares at me a moment before she goes on.

"So if ya don't have any objections, I am gonna get a flight ta Norway instead of the States."

I'm not sure what to say at first. I've never flown on a plane all by myself before, but then I had never done a lot of things by myself before this trip. I figure, as long as I know where the puke bag is before I take off, I'll be just fine. Then I start thinking more about my dad and my throat gets tight and I have to concentrate hard so I don't cry.

"I think you're right, Grandma. I would bet all the tea in China that they aren't telling us everything. I'm glad you're going to Norway because I want you to find out what happened to my dad."

Grandma Agee looks at me with a puzzled look on her face.

"Ya want *me* to find out? Agnes, I need a resourceful and intelligent person ta help me on this quest, and after our trip ta Turkey, I think you're just the girl I'm lookin' for."

I don't know what else to do but stare at my grandmother. *Is she pulling my leg?* Of course, I don't think she actually has hold of my leg and is tugging on it. It's another one of those idioms, one I know without having to look it up in the idiom book at the library. It means *to play a joke on or tease someone.*

"You want me to come to Norway with you?"

"I do," she says with a smile. "We'd have ta get your mother's okay, but it doesn't make sense to cross the pond twice. We should really just head ta Norway from here."

"Cross the pond?"

"The Atlantic Ocean."

"How are we going to get an okay from Mom? We're going to the airport now!"

Grandma doesn't bat an eye. "We fly ta Norway and send her a telegram from there. Easier ta ask for forgiveness than permission, I always say."

"You do?"

Grandma Agee raises her eyebrows and tilts her head in way of an answer.

I won't have time or a library to help me prepare for this trip like I normally would, but I'm lucky enough to find a travel guide to Scandinavia, which is all the countries in that area of the world: Norway, Sweden, Finland, Denmark, and Iceland, at a bookstore in the airport before we board the plane.

Once we're inside the plane, I buckle myself in, pull out my Scandinavian travel guide, and start my preparations.

Grandma Agee touches my leg.

"Agnes. I told ya that your father worked for the Central Intelligence Agency, but what I didn't tell ya is what he did for the CIA." Grandma hesitates. She looks like she's not sure she should tell me this.

"Ya know, he could've had many jobs there. He could'a worked in an office. He could'a trained people. He could've even worked in security, say, watching over President Kennedy or some other government hot shot."

My eyebrows go up in amazement. That would be really cool if my dad helped protect President Kennedy!

"Is that what he did, Grandma? Was he a security officer in the CIA?"

Grandma shakes her head and has the most serious look on her face. "There was somethin' else that Nero Bahar told me about your father after we left you all yellow-faced at the spice shop. Somethin' that might explain why Mr. Brooks and even Mr. Bahar couldn't tell us much and why the government lied to us. I also think it might well have a bearing on what happened to him."

My book has snapped closed. My grandmother has my full attention.

"Agnes, your father worked in espionage."

I give my grandmother a confused look.

"He was a spy."

A letter from Agnes

Hello Reader,
    I thought you'd like to know a few of the definitions and idioms I left out of my story because I thought it would make it too hard to read. You might know some of them already but just in case, I wanted to save you some time and look them up for you. Now that my mom gave me a pocket dictionary, I can look up words a lot easier.
    The first one is on page one: <u>moot - not worth talking about, no longer important or worth discussing</u>. Did you know that one? It's a weird word but it's fun to say.
    Two of the figures of speech, which I later found out are called idioms, on page twenty-two might be hard to figure out. I found them when I was looking at the idiom book in the library.
    (<u>Idiom</u> is a strange word itself, so I looked it up in the dictionary. The dictionary said an idiom is <u>an expression that cannot be understood from the meanings of its separate</u>

words but that has a separate meaning of its own. That sounded like gibberish to me, so I asked a librarian and she explained that the words in an idiom don't usually have anything to do with its real meaning. That makes more sense. Don't you agree?)

Six of one, half dozen of another - you probably know that one. Your mom or dad might say it when they are arguing with each other about which way to drive to Grandma's house.

Pot calling the kettle black - I asked Grandma Agee about this one. You have to remember that pots used to be mostly black because people cooked over fire, so a pot (which is black) calling a kettle (which is also black) black, means one person is saying something about another person that they themselves do or are like. Imagine a friend, who is eating a donut, tells you that you shouldn't eat too much sugar.

That's neither here nor there - it means it's unimportant or not related to what you're talking about. It would be as if your teacher is telling the class how to dress on a field trip to our state's capitol, in Madison, and a boy asks if it's okay if he can bring a snack.

On page thirty-two I use the idiom, <u>right up your alley</u>, when I'm talking about my brother Max and how he likes to get out of work. It means <u>that's just the kind of thing the person is into</u>.

Another idiom I use (on page forty-two) is <u>tool around</u>. I would guess you can figure out what it means because I'm talking about Grandma Barb's car — <u>to drive around in</u> — but I tried to find out where it came from and I couldn't. If you figure it out, let me know, would you?

I use the word <u>circumstances</u> on page sixty-four, which means <u>a condition or fact that effects a certain situation</u>, when I'm talking about how sometimes I get into trouble by no fault of my own. You'd have to agree, my bee pin falling out of my hair wasn't my fault. Things like that just seem to happen to me. Does that happen to you, too? I use the word <u>conspire</u>, too, a bit farther down the page. That means <u>to secretly plan with someone to do something that is harmful or illegal.</u> It sure seemed to me that something was conspiring to get me into trouble with my Grandmother that day. Luckily it turned out okay, and the pie my pin fell into tasted kind of good, too!

When the tour guide in the Hagia Sophia was telling us about one of the mosaics, he said the picture was <u>depicting</u> [<u>v: showing someone or something in a picture, painting or photograph</u>] four important people, at least they were important to whoever made the mosaic. Do you remember who the four people were?

When my Grandma asks me to get us a table in the hotel restaurant so she can talk to the man from the consulate, I say that this request is <u>odder than an eight-dollar bill.</u> I know you can figure out what that idiom means. My dad used to say that, so I wanted to put it in my story.

I also thought you might like to know a bit about typhus, even though you'll probably never get that disease. After our trip, I took some time to look it up. Typhus is bacteria that you get from lice or fleas, so that's why the soldiers in the WWI book I was reading had it. They were living in very bad conditions where they couldn't get clean for a long time. Typhus is uncommon in the US, but if you normally complain to your mom when she says you have to take a bath, you better just go ahead the take it.

Have any of you heard the saying (another idiom) <u>I'll be a monkey's uncle</u>? I say this when Grandma tries to trick me into thinking she's going to meet someone to buy a rug when I know she's going to the US Consulate. It means that the likelihood of her buying a rug is about as likely as me being an uncle to a monkey. It also can mean that someone is surprised. It's pretty funny, I think. I wonder who came up with some of these idioms.

And I wanted to make sure I told you that even though I thought (and so did my mom and grandma) that aspirin is okay for kids, it might not be. It has been associated with something called Reye Syndrome. So if your mom or dad wants to give you an aspirin for a fever, tell them to read this.

You might have heard the word foil [v: to prevent (someone) from doing something or achieving a goal] in the cartoons, or something but you might not have known what it means. That's why I put the definition here, just in case. It's another cool word that you can use when you're writing an essay for school. It will really impress your teacher.

Here's another one: sparse [adj: present only in small amounts]. I say this when I'm explaining what Yusuf's house looks like. I guess you figured out that Yusuf's family doesn't have much money. That still doesn't explain why Yusuf never combs his hair. I guess he's like most of the boys I know; he doesn't care much about what he looks like.

Did you get the meaning of the idiom I use on page one hundred and twenty-nine? You can't judge a book by its cover. It means you can't judge something or someone just by how it/they looks/look on the outside. That's not always easy to do, but Yusuf really taught me that lesson.

I don't know if any of you have been around sheep much, but the noise a sheep makes is called a bleat. It really is like the sound your parents made when they were trying to teach you what a sheep sounded like. For fun, go up to them and ask them what a sheep sounds like. I bet they'll do it for you!

The last idiom I put in the book was when Grandma Agee told me she was taking me to Norway. (Cool, huh?!) She didn't <u>bat an eye</u> - <u>didn't hesitate or react</u> - when she said she'd tell my mom where we were after we got there. Kind of sneaky for a grandmother. I think that's why I'm really getting to like her and because she wants to find out what happened to my dad.

Were you as surprised as I was that my dad was a spy? I had no clue and I lived with him for twelve years! I wonder if my mom knows. That explains why he traveled to places like England and Turkey and Russia. I guess he was in Norway too but didn't tell us. I wonder what he did there. I'll let you know when I find out!

Your friend,
Agnes Kelly

p.s. If you are wondering why my penmanship is so neat, I will remind you, I go to a Catholic grade school. Those nuns don't fool around when it comes to penmanship!

Acknowledgments

I have quite a few people to thank for their help on this book.

My readers (in alphabetical order): Kristina Anderson, Valerie Biel, Ignacia Boersma, Andrew Craven, Rachel Craven, Tyler Durst, Sophie Gryske, Dolores Kester, Lorna Lee, Erica Loeffelholtz, Maya Merchant, Jill Peterson, Kathy Schleif, Sara Smith and her daughter, and Evan Weinstock.

As usual, my brother Earl Keleny (earlkeleny.com) helped me with my cover. I did it completely myself this time but not without quite a bit of hand-holding and suggestions from the real artist in the family.

Thank you all so much! I couldn't have done this without you.

About the Author

First, I want to thank Agnes for letting me write her story. It was fun to write and fun to read. She is a nice girl and she thought it would be okay for me to tell you a bit about myself.

Strangely enough, I didn't read much when I was in school. When I went to school, my teachers always had stories I was required to read, which weren't the kind of books I liked, so I just kind of gave up on the idea of reading, I guess.

When I was done with college, I started to read again. Now I read all the time. Actually, I usually have a couple books going: one I listen to in my car and one I read wherever I'm at. Agnes and I have that in common; I often bring a book with me if I know I am going to be sitting around waiting.

But, of course, I can't read all the time; I also have a job, but I'm lucky in that my job is also related to books. I run a publishing company called CKBooks Publishing. I help other people with whatever they need to help them write and eventually publish their own books. That's how Agnes and I got connected. It's a fun job for me.

Along with reading and working at my publishing company, I also write. If you want to see all the books I have written so far or if you want to learn a bit more about me, you can go to christinekelenybooks. com. Or you can check out Agnes' own website: AgnesKellyMysteryAdventures.com. That is also where I have a Readers' Group sign up, if you want to be one of my special readers.

If you want to see what I do with my publishing company, you can go to ckbookspublishing.com.

Thanks for reading Agnes' first story and I hope you enjoy Book II in the Agnes Kelly Mystery Adventure Series, as well!

~ Christine

p.s. If you liked this story, and you are old enough, please leave a review on your favorite website. Reviews are the lifeblood of all authors (meaning they are as important to my writing as blood is in our bodies), especially independently published authors such as myself. ☺

Thank you!